Len Deighton was born in London in 1929. He worked as a railway clerk before doing his National Service in the RAF as a photographer attached to the Special Investigation Branch.

After his discharge in 1949, he went to art school – first to the St Martin's School of Art, and then to the Royal College of Art on a scholarship. It was while working as a waiter in the evenings that he developed an interest in cookery – a subject he was later to make his own in an animated strip for the *Observer* and in two cookery books. He worked for a while as an illustrator in New York and as art director of an advertising agency in London.

Deciding it was time to settle down, Deighton moved to the Dordogne where he started work on his first book, *The Ipcress File*. Published in 1962, the book was an immediate and spectacular success. Since then he has written twenty-four books of fiction and non-fiction – including spy stories, and highly researched war novels and histories – all of which have appeared to international acclaim.

1987 marks the twenty-fifth anniversary of the first publication of Len Deighton's THE IPCRESS FILE, the novel that simultaneously revolutionized the espionage-thriller genre and marked the arrival on the fiction scene of one of the most powerful narrative talents in Twentieth Century literature.

Grafton Books is proud to present special Silver Jubilee editions of the major works of Len Deighton to celebrate the first quarter-century of his spectacularly successful writing career. All the books in the Len Deighton Silver Jubilee collection carry special forewords by the author exclusive to these editi⟨...⟩ these limited editions a⟨...⟩ accomplished writers of⟨...⟩

By the same author

The Ipcress File
Horse Under Water
Funeral in Berlin
Billion-Dollar Brain
An Expensive Place to Die
Only When I Larf
Bomber
Close-Up
Spy Story
Yesterday's Spy
Twinkle, Twinkle, Little Spy
SS-GB
XPD
Goodbye Mickey Mouse
Berlin Game
Mexico Set
London Match

Action Cookbook
Basic French Cooking (revised and enlarged
   from *Où est le Garlic?*)

Fighter
Airshipwreck
Blitzkrieg
The Battle of Britain

SILVER JUBILEE EDITION

LEN DEIGHTON

Declarations of War

TRIAD
GRAFTON BOOKS

LONDON GLASGOW
TORONTO SYDNEY AUCKLAND

Triad
Grafton Books
8 Grafton Street, London W1X 3LA

Published by Triad Grafton Books 1981
Reprinted 1983, 1984
Silver Jubilee Edition 1987

Triad Paperbacks Ltd is an imprint of
Chatto, Bodley Head & Jonathan Cape Ltd and
Grafton Books, A Division of the Collins Publishing Group

First published in Great Britain by
Jonathan Cape Ltd 1971

ISBN 0-586-07412-0

Printed and bound in Great Britain by
Collins, Glasgow

Set in Times

Preface

As I told my publisher, *Declarations of War* is not a book of short stories. Books of short stories contain old bits of writing culled from ancient magazines or newspapers, and assembled together with little more than their author in common.

Declarations of War (with the exception of one story that had been published elsewhere) was written in one go, from start to finish. I had always tried to write so that each chapter of any book could stand alone. I'd always believed that a book should be a collection of 'short stories', written and arranged in such a way that the reader who reads it right the way through is left with a complete impression of the author's initial idea. It's not easy to do, of course and I wouldn't claim that I have ever succeeded. But in *Declarations of War* I took the opportunity to try this in another more extreme way.

My chapters – I'll have to call them stories, I suppose – are about heroes and heroism. But the heroes of my stories are not made of the stuff of heroes. There is the jaded firing squad commander, the out-moded general, the fighter pilot fighting for the wrong side, the arms salesman, the nervous young flyer, the boorish tank man who is insensitive to everything except his tank and the unheroic little immigrant sergeant Winkelstein who discovers suddenly that he possesses the power of life and death over his men, and allows them to see it too.

It was of course a joy to research. The flora and fauna of the US Civil War kept me happily reading for two days. The psychological reaction of RAF aircrew to stress was the result of many enjoyable social evenings with Dr Stafford Clark, an expert on the subject. I discovered something of the flying characteristics of the Sopwith Camel and that the colour of German anti-aircraft gun smoke differed from that of the British guns. I was fortunate in finding an eye-witness account of a military execution so that the Indian story is very close to the historical truth of that strange episode.

Only with the story 'It Must Have Been Two Other Fellows' did I go badly wrong. I believe it's the worst mistake in research I've made so far (and if you know a worse one be so kind as to not write and tell me). Choosing carefully the sort of armoured vehicle that a man could become obsessed with took time, and provided me with an excuse to talk to many ex-tankers. The Sherman Firefly fitted the bill beautifully. I was equally careful about the Italian background with its specific slang and jargon. But too late I discovered that the Sherman Firefly was developed for the Normandy campaign. They were never used in Italy. Ah, well.

It is a book of locations: a big delapidated country house, a cramped room in an old university, the temperamental sky, the jungle. It is a pleasure – and a self-indulgence – to use so many of them but I had done this in other books. I think it was Raymond Chandler who said that when he didn't know what to do next (with his plot) he had someone come through the door carrying a gun. I was going through a period when even my most loyal readers might have suspected that when I didn't know what to do next I moved to another location.

But the freedom to move from subject to subject, as I have in this book, is the ultimate freedom for the author. At the end of it I knew why so many writers grieved that the market for short stories had died so completely.

And yet I discovered many myths too. It is simply not

true that unsuccessful ideas for novels can be used for short stories. Neither is it true that a wonderful idea for a short story can be expanded into a book. Although it's always possible, of course, to write one of those stories that has neither beginning or end: the author producing it like a haberdasher selling some yards from a bolt of cloth. But a well-constructed short story can only exist as that.

I was particularly appalled when my American publisher (an Englishman in fact) decided to omit two stories from the US edition. He wouldn't have done that to a book. But all publishers hate short stories. I'm sure they don't hate reading them but publishers are convinced that readers don't like them. One publisher told me that, when deciding the print run, an average book of short stories is estimated to sell half of what a fiction book by the same author will do. Is it a self-fulfilling prophecy? Do readers really hate short stories in book form? Perhaps publishers and authors have only themselves to blame for putting together too many ill-assorted collections of old odds and ends.

But publishers cannot be blamed for the demise of the short story. It was the magazines that kept the short story alive. Not just the big fat wealthy US magazines that paid enough per word to attract Hemingway and Scott Fitzgerald but smaller unpretentious journals – many of them London based – that encouraged new writing. Now such magazines are long dead. I find them sometimes, mixed with the junk in flea markets, and I read them with delight and admiration. Television has replaced the short story, I'm told. I look at TV and I can't help feeling just a bit sorry.

And I found when writing this book that it wasn't possible to keep exactly to my plan. I couldn't write a book consisting of disparate chapters. By the time I was finished, *Declarations of War* was a collection of short stories distinguished only by being written as part of one plan at one time.

It's the restriction on characterization that makes the difference. Perhaps next time I try, I'll keep the same characters in each chapter. And perhaps there shouldn't be as many different locations, or differences of period in which they are set.

But then, that would be just an ordinary book, wouldn't it?

Len Deighton, 1986

Contents

It Must Have Been Two Other Fellows   1
Winter's Morning   29
First Base   45
Paper Casualty   63
Brent's Deus Ex Machina   79
A New Way To Say Goodnight   92
Lord Nick Flies Again   102
Discipline   111
Mission Control: Hannibal One   127
Adagio   136
Bonus for a Salesman   151
Action   174
Twelve Good Men and True   184

It Must Have Been Two Other Fellows

James Sidney Pelling was fifty-nine years old. Ever since his cadet days he had been obsessed with motor-cars. He now had four: a brand-new Bentley, a battered DB6, a Land-Rover for the farm and a Cooper S that his new blower and modified carburettors would convert into the most exciting car of all.

For a job as complex as this he needed the electronic tuning bench at the Hillside Garage. They were Colonel Pelling's tenants – he owned all the land between the farm and the Salisbury road – and the owners gave him the use of the work-shop on Sundays.

On this particular Sunday, cook had sent him sandwiches and a Thermos of coffee. He'd hardly touched them, working right through lunchtime. By three in the afternoon he was almost finished and was watching the timing on the neon strobe when a car bumped over the rubber strips that rang a bell in the office. Pelling ignored it. Anyone who failed to see the huge CLOSED notice on the pumps shouldn't be permitted behind the wheel of a car, in Pelling's opinion. There was the imperious toot-de-toot of an Italian power horn. It sounded again, and Pelling decided that the driver must be told to go away. He wiped his hands on a piece of cotton waste.

As he entered the cashier's glass-fronted box, he noticed that it was raining heavily. He reached for the ancient raincoat and hat that were kept behind the door and buttoned the torn collar tight around his throat.

He could always distinguish a salesman's car: new, cheap and fast, well-worn by heavy driving and scratched

1

from careless parking. The driver had an expense-account plumpness. He sat behind the wheel in a drip-dry shirt, while the jacket of his shiny Dacron-mixture suit was on a hanger in the rear window. It was still swinging gently from the abrupt braking.

'Come on, Dad,' said the driver with a sigh.

Before Pelling could think of a reply the man was out of the car and advancing upon him, smiling the smile that only successful salesmen produce so quickly. 'Colonel Pelling,' he said. 'Colonel Pelling. Well, I'll be buggered, begging your pardon, sir.'

'I'm sorry.' said Pelling stiffly. 'You have the advantage of me . . .'

'Wool. You can't go wrong with me next to the skin.' He laughed.

'Wool?'

'My little joke, Colonel.' He stood to attention in a burlesque of military obedience. 'Wool; W-o-o-l, Corporal Wool 397, sir! Royal Welsh Greys, D Squadron, No 1 Troop. From Tunisia all the way to Florence. Best years of my life, in a way. Place me now, sir?'

Pelling tried to make this over-fed, middle-aged man into a young corporal. He failed.

'The farmhouse on the hill,' prompted Wool, 'near Sergeant-Major village.'

The Colonel still looked puzzled and Wool said, 'Oh well, it must have been two other fellows, eh?' He laughed and repeated his joke slowly. When he spoke again his voice was loud and a little exasperated. 'Don't tell me you've forgotten the farmhouse. When the Tedeschi nearly clobbered the whole mob of us, and we sat there like lemons?'

'Of course,' said Pelling,'you were the fellow with the Bren. I remember him quite differently . . .'

'No, no, no,' said Wool. 'That was a bloke named

2

Stephens. He got the MM for that. That was the following week.'

'Corporal Wool, yes . . .'

'Lance-jack at the time, actually. Ended up a sergeant though: temporary, acting, unpaid.' He smiled and saluted.

'Wool,' said Pelling. 'It's good to see you again. You're looking well and prosperous.'

Wool grinned and tucked his shirt into his waistband. 'It always comes loose when I'm driving. Yeah, well, I'm not bad, how are you?'

'I'm well, in fact very well.'

Wool shook his head doubtfully and stared into Pelling's face. 'You're not looking too good, Colonel, if you don't mind an ex-lance-jack saying so.'

'I'm just a bit tired,' said Pelling. He smiled at Wool's concern. 'I've been working since eight o'clock this morning.'

'Here?'

'Yes.'

'Christ!' He looked around the rain-swept forecourt. It was grimy and littered with ice-cream tubs. A sign said: FREE WITH 4 GALLONS OF PETROL, A PACKET OF BALLOONS.

'A packet of bleeding balloons,' said Wool. 'All these petrol companies are the same: free bloody hair-brushes or free bloody wine-glasses. What they want to offer is a free bloody service: top up the battery, check the water and tyre pressures. I'll bet you never wipe the wind-screens, do you?'

'No, I don't.'

'Exactly. Here,' he grabbed at Pelling's sleeve, 'you own this place?'

'I'm afraid not.'

Wool sniffed and nodded to himself. 'It's a rotten

3

shame, that's all I can say. You were the youngest-looking Colonel any of us had ever seen – a chestful of gongs, and a good bringing-up, it's a bloody disgrace. There's your Socialist governments for you. Here, I'm getting wet, jump in out of this rain.' Wool reached for *The Times* and put two sheets of it upon the plastic seat before opening the door for Pelling.

'Colonel Pelling,' said Wool, looking at him closely and imprinting the memory of this moment upon his mind. 'Colonel Pelling.'

Wool twisted round in his seat and found a packet of cheroots in his jacket. He tore off its cellophane wrapping and opened it with a flourish. 'Have a cigar?'

'Thank you, Wool, no. I've given up smoking.'

'It's a rich man's hobby now,' agreed Wool. He put the cheroots away and took from the glove compartment a Havana in a metal container. He used a cigar-cutter to prepare it, and lit it with enough ceremony to demonstrate that he was a man familar with good living. He exhaled the smoke slowly and turned to face the ex-Colonel with a calm happiness.

The Colonel had aged well; no surplus fat or heavy jowls. His nose was bony and his jaw was hard. He was lean and tall, just as Wool remembered him, except that the hair below his oily hat was almost white. Wool looked at Pelling's hands. His dirty skin was tanned and leathery, just as one would expect of a man who spent long hours out in all weathers slaving at the petrol pumps.

Wool, on the other hand, was not so easy to identify with the nineteen-year-old Corporal that the Colonel had briefly known. Florid, and wearing large fashionable black-framed spectacles, he was like any one of the dozens of commercials who filled up at the Hillside before the non-stop race back to London. On his finger there

4

was a signet ring and on his wrist a complex watch and a gold identity bracelet.

It must have been two other fellows, thought Pelling. Yes, as soldiers they had been saints or hooligans, torturers or rescuers, but none survived. Those that eventually became civilians were different men.

Pelling looked at the interior of the car. No doubt about it being cherished and cared for, even if it wasn't done to Pelling's taste. The steering-wheel had a leather cover, the seats were covered in imitation leopard-skin and a baby's shoe dangled from the mirror. There was a St Christopher bolted to the dashboard and in the rear window there was a large plastic dog that nodded and two cushions with the registration number boldly knitted into their design.

'Seen any of your blokes?' asked Wool.

'Not recently,' said Pelling.

'I've never been to an Old Comrades or anything.'

'Nor have I,' said Pelling. 'I'm not much use at that sort of thing.'

Wool looked at the filthy raincoat. 'I understand,' he said. He studied the ash of his cigar. 'The funny thing was that you only came up to the farmhouse for a look-see, didn't you?'

'I'm only here for a shufti, Lieutenant.' The subaltern looked at the man crawling in through the door. The newcomer's rank badges were unmistakable, and yet he looked younger than the thirty-year-old Lieutenant. 'You came on foot, sir?'

'Jeeped up the wadi.'

'Corporal. Crawl out and move the Colonel's Jeep into the barn out of sight.'

'There's eight gallons of water in it for you,' said Pelling, 'and a crate of beer for your chaps.'

'That will cheer them up, sir.'

5

'It won't cheer them up much,' said Pelling. 'It's that gnats'-pee from Tunis. Psychological warfare by the temperance people, I'd say.'

The Lieutenant rubbed his unshaven chin and nodded his thanks as the Corporal went out into the yard and started to move the Jeep.

'It's stupid of me,' said Pelling. 'I didn't realize they could see as far as the truck.'

'They've got a new OP on the east slope of the big tit – Point 401 that is – we only noticed it yesterday, my sergeant saw a bit of movement there. Can't be sure it's manned all the time.'

'It was stupid of me,' repeated Pelling.

The Lieutenant had seldom spoken with colonels and certainly not one who'd admit to stupidity. Awkwardly he said, 'Would you like to go up to the loft, sir? Sloan, get brewing. And open that tin of milk.'

The Colonel held the field glasses delicately, as though he was taking the pulse of two black-metal wrists. From the loft he could see more than ten miles along the valley. It was noon. The sunbaked hills were misty green puddings, surmounted by outcrops of grey rock and ringed by precarious terraces of crops. The olive groves lower down were plagued with the black festering sores of artillery fire, and untended vegetables had run to seed. Nowhere was there any movement of man or machine, nor were there horses or mules, cattle, sheep or goats – at least, no live ones. Pelling searched carefully along the German lines from where the River Caro was no more than a piddle of dirty water meandering through the high-banked wadi, to the ruins of 'Sergeant-Major', as the troops had renamed the village of Santa Maria Maggiore. If it hadn't been for the cowshed at the far end of the yard, and the abandoned Churchill tank fifty yards behind it, he'd have been able to see the hills beyond the river, and the main road that led eventually to Rome. He studied the road carefully: dust hung above it like incense smoke, and yet he could see no transport there. From somewhere far away a church bell began tolling an inexpert rhythm.

'A dedicated priest,' said Pelling, still looking through the glasses. Then he lowered them and began to wipe the lenses. He used a white linen handkerchief, rough-dried and unpressed and mottled with the faint stains of ancient dirt.

'Partisans, more likely. They use the bells as signals to regroup.' He passed the Colonel a handkerchief of khaki silk. Bought by a loving mother for a newly commissioned son, thought Pelling as he finished polishing the binoculars. Handling the smelly glasses with exaggerated care, Pelling put them into the battered leather case and gave them back to the Lieutenant.

'Your people will be coming tomorrow, sir?'

'Yes, we'll get rid of that tank and cowshed for you.' He said it like a surgeon about to amputate, and like a humane surgeon he tried to give the impression that it would make things better.

'That will give us quite a view,' said the Lieutenant. Pelling nodded. They both knew that it would make the farm such a good observation point that then the Germans would also want it. Very badly.

'Our attack can't be far off now,' said the Lieutenant, seeking reassurance. Pelling said nothing. Allied HQ didn't tell engineer colonels their plans, any more than they told infantry subalterns. They told the one to clear fields of fire and the other to shoot.

Pelling said, 'In another three or four weeks the autumn rains will make that valley into a bog. Do you know what rain does to that dusty soil?' It was a rhetorical question; the Lieutenant's face, hair, hands and uniform – like everyone else's – were coloured grey by the same abrasive powder that got in the guns and the tea.

'Yes,' said the Lieutenant. The attack would be soon.

What sort of man would build a farm up here on the side of Monte Nuovo: a fool or an aesthete, or both. The wind screamed constantly, the cloud was almost close enough to touch and the trees were stunted and hunch-backed; but the view was like a Francesca painting. Back in Pelling's part of the world men built their houses low.

In war, though, it was the villages in the valleys that survived best. Houses and churches on high ground were invariably destroyed as the armies fought for observation points. There was a moral there somewhere, thought Pelling, but he was too tired to deduce it.

'What will you do after the war, Lieutenant?' Pelling sipped the hot sweet tea that was heavy with the smell of condensed milk.

'Oh, I don't know.' This was a new sort of conversation and he spoke in a different voice and omitted the 'sir'. 'I always wanted to be a vet – I'm keen on animals – but I'll be too old to start studying by the time this lot's over. Probably I'll just take over the old man's antique shop. And you?'

At first the Lieutenant was afraid that he'd offended the young Colonel. With an MC and DSO and a colonel's rank at his age, perhaps he felt that there was no other world but the army. To soften it a little the Lieutenant said, 'You're a regular, of course.'

Pelling grinned, 'Yes, Woolwich, Staff College, the lot. I'm about as regular as you can get.'

'I suppose this is . . . to us it's the worst sort of interruption to our lives, but I suppose for you it's the thing you've been waiting for.'

'All you War Service types think that,' said Pelling, 'but if you think that any regular soldier likes fighting

8

wars, you're quite wrong.' He saw the Lieutenant glance at his badges. 'Oh, we get promotion, but only at the expense of having our nice little club invaded by a lot of amateurs who don't want to be there. The peacetime army is quite a different show. A chap doesn't go into that in the hope that there will eventually be a war.'

'No, I suppose not.'

'You won't believe it,' said Pelling, 'but peacetime soldiering can be good fun, especially for a youngster straight from school. The army's so small that one gets to know everyone. One travels a lot, and there's ample leave as well as polo, cricket and rugger. It's not at all bad, Lieutenant, believe me. Even the parade ground can have a curious satisfaction.'

'The parade ground?'

'A thousand men, perfectly still and silent . . . and able to move in precise unison. Professional dancers probably share the same elation.'

'Like marching behind a military band? We did that once, passing out of OCTU.'

'That's a part of it, but for me a silent parade ground has even more of a ritualistic effect. The body moves and yet the mind remains. There is a separation of physical and spiritual self that can liberate the mind like nothing else I know.'

'Are you a Buddhist, sir?' It was a reckless guess.

'Once I nearly was,' admitted Pelling.

'And now?'

'I am slowly rediscovering Christianity.'

Pelling had told no one about the time he'd spent billeted in the monastery near Naples, of the long conversations he'd had with the Abbot, arguing so fiercely that at times they were both yelling. Apart from his driver no one knew of the trips to the slum villages, and not even

9

the driver could have guessed the effect that time had had upon him. 'I'm going into a monastery,' said Pelling.

'Really?' He stared at the Colonel, trying to see some strange secret.

Pelling nodded. He did not doubt that he would go back to the great white building with its orchards and its library and the life that went on without interruption for century after century. It was arranged that he would get both the tractors going again and find or build a lorry that would take the produce into Naples where they would get a better price for their vegetables.

There had been times during the fighting when only the promise of a cloistered life kept Colonel James Pelling going. He visualized himself thirty years hence; stouter than Father Franco and quieter than Father Mario – and perhaps less devout than either. Yet, as the old man had explained, the Order had in the past received men with doubts, and some of these had become its most valuable sons. Would one ever get used to being called 'Father James', Pelling wondered.

'Do you believe there is a heaven for tractors, Father James?'

'If there isn't, Brother, then Father James will not go there.' They were truly good, those simple men.

'Would you be able to stand that?' It was the Lieutenant speaking. 'The quiet: I'd go bonkers.'

'It's not a silent order,' said Pelling.

'You've no family then?'

'A father.' He'd go – what was the word the Lieutenant had used? – bonkers. Yes, he'd go bonkers all right. But Pelling was determined not to repeat the mistakes of his father's solitary life. Days in the boat yard or at the drawing-board, lunch in the pub with the works manager. Dinner in the yacht club, or a late snack left by cook: dry ham sandwiches clamped under a plate. And what was the purpose of his father's life: a couple of knots gained by hull modifications, a win at Cowes, a telegram from a transatlantic cup winner. That wasn't enough for him, not nearly enough. Pelling could hear the soldiers below talking about what they would do with their lives after the war.

'Mr Steeple, sir.' It was Wool's voice calling softly, 'Two Marks IVs turning off the road near the track at two o'clock.'

Lieutenant Steeple said, 'Sergeant Manley, get your sniper's rifle. Have a go at their visors. You never know, you might star his periscope glass.'

The Lieutenant was too late grabbing for the glasses. 'They've stopped,' grunted Pelling. He rubbed the lenses with a handkerchief and then looked again. 'Nice hull-down position if they were going to batter us.' Their guns hadn't traversed, so it was difficult to know whether they were covering the main road or the farmhouse to the east of it. The lieutenant picked pieces of straw from his duty battle-dress blouse while he waited for the next move.

'You should wear denims,' said Pelling without taking the glasses from his eyes. 'That rough battle-dress material picks up straw and stuff.' He couldn't see very well, for the morning sun reflected on the dry, dusty soil so that it shimmered as he remembered the desert had done.

'No, no, no, sir,' interrupted Wool. He chuckled and flicked ash from his cigar. 'It wasn't hot and sunny, it was a close overcast day. There had been rain that morning. Not the sort of rain we got a few weeks later, but rain. And it wasn't morning, it was late afternoon when the German tanks arrived, very late, almost dark. You were in the cellar drinking tea with that Mr Steeple, the officer. I came down the cellar steps and said, "Any more tea for anyone? There are a couple of Tedeschi tanks outside the front door."'

11

'Damn!' shouted Steeple. Pelling looked around for a place to stand his mug of tea and then decided to drink it hurriedly. It scalded his mouth. Pelling let Steeple up the steps first. It was his show, but Pelling couldn't resist interfering.

'Radio?' called Pelling.

'Bishop!' yelled Steeple. 'Tell Company: Two Ted Mark IVs moving in on us fast.' He looked at Pelling and said more calmly, 'No, wait a minute, make that: Two Mark IVs, range nine hundred, bearing oh three five.'

Everyone stood very quietly listening to the radio operator patiently repeating the message. Only Pelling and Steeple could see the two enemy tanks. The others were just staring very hard at the wall and the rafters, as if by opening their eyes wide they would be able to hear better. It must have been three or four minutes before anyone spoke and then Wool said, 'Listen to that nightingale sing! It's as clear as a glass of Worthington . . .'

'Couldn't have been mē,' chuckled Wool. 'I couldn't tell a nightingale from a budgerigar; still can't.' He puffed his cigar. 'What I do remember, though, is you making us black our faces with soot from the stove. Regular Sioux war party we looked.'

Wool had often played Red Indians when he stayed with his Gran. Blacking his face was an important part of that. He'd take his uncle's boat and row along the stream. Using the oar against the river-bed, he could push himself right in among the reeds so that he and the boat disappeared. The cars on the road to Bishopsbridge were stage coaches, but pedestrians were miners and no honourable Indian brave would scalp them.

'Did I?' said Pelling.

'Yes, it was after the rations came up that night. You nearly put Bishop on a charge when he said the soot would make no difference in the dark. You called him a young lout, I remember. He was a family man, too. He was real choked about that.'

'None of them were louts,' said Pelling. 'They were good chaps.'

'But that Keats was a dodgy one. He'd done three years for duffing up a policeman at a Cup Final in 1936. Sergeant Manley was a bit nervous of Keats. Never gave him any dirty jobs or anything dangerous.'

'Was Keats the Scots lad that tried to get back along the ditch?'

'That's him; short thickset bloke with bad teeth.'

'It was a brave thing to do.'

'Brave?' said Wool. 'He was trying to give himself up to old Ted. He was off to surrender, thought he was going to get killed.'

'You think so?'

Keats put his rifle to rest against the broken stove and then crouched by the window waiting for a break in the mortar fire. He went over the windowsill so skilfully that few men saw him go.

Like a burglar, reflected Pelling, yes, like a burglar.

'Rifle grenades, not mortars,' said Wool. 'You taught me the different sound of those. Like a champagne cork popping, the two-inch mortar, you said. Mind you, I'd never heard a bottle of champers pop at that time.' He laughed to remember his youth. 'And it was a Sherman tank, not a Churchill.'

'What makes you think that Keats was trying to surrender?'

'He was carrying a piece of bed-sheet. It was tucked into the front of his blouse. When the burial party got up to him next day they thought he must be an old one – you know, swollen up with the sun – but it was a sheet.'

'Poor fellow.'

'Yes. Kept us going all night, didn't he. Screaming and

13

carrying on. Mona or Rhona or something. He was probably only nicked at first, if he'd kept quiet he would have been all right perhaps. Stephens tried to shoot him once, you know. It was too dark.'

Why had Wool chosen to remember it like that? Had the new fashion in embittered war films and stories persuaded Wool to distort the reality of his memory in favour of the more fashionable rubbish of writers who had not been there? Wool had been a hero: young, pimply, foolish and brave.

'I'd like to have a go,' said Wool.

'It's up to the Colonel,' said Lieutenant Steeple. No one had to ask what Wool was volunteering for.

'By all means,' said Pelling. Already the valleys were dark, and the last glimmer of sunlight lit the church on the mountaincrest facing them.

'I'll go out the front,' said Wool. 'That's where they'll least expect me. I'll make towards the Sherman in front of us and then work round to the tracks, keeping well away from the house. I'll see if I can spot Keats, too.'

Lieutenant Steeple said, 'Sergeant Manley, we'll put some phosphorus grenades into the wadi end of the track. Make a rumpus while the Corporal gets clear.' To Wool he added, 'Keats is probably done for, don't take any risks to bring him back.'

Pelling said, 'Corporal, if you are spotted, lie low. We'll tickle them up to give you a chance. If you need to come back to us, come in on a line with the barn. We'll be extra careful on that bearing.'

The dark was like playing Red Indians, too. He'd crept up on the bison in Mr Jones's field. Sometimes he'd be within touching distance before it ran away bleating. When he got out of the army he'd go back to Gran's. He liked it in the country; Bell Street was a dirty place, without grass or trees or anywhere that kids could play.

14

When he had kids they would have the countryside to play in. They'd row out into the reeds, as he had done, and catch fish and help old Mr Jones herd the Jerseys and carry the milk.

Hold it, there's the tank right ahead. A Sherman Firefly with Cindy Four painted on it in red letters, that's the one. It was just like being a Red Indian, except that the ground was cold and damp and the cowboys were using two-inch mortars and Mark IVs. His bloody knee! There was a stink of ancient dung and fresh human excreta, but the wet grass had a smell that he liked. Careful of the wire.

What sort of job could he get in the country? None that would bring much money, but then one didn't need so much money in the country. Gran would let him have the room in the loft and there'd be agricultural training courses for ex-servicemen. He'd asked the Education Officer. Now that he knew Wool was serious he'd promised to get the papers about it from Division.

'Did you ever think about one of those security organizations?' said Wool. 'Still, you're not as fast on your pins as you used to be. They'd probably not want a bloke as old as you are. You might prove a bit of a liability up against a gang of toughs using ammonia and pickaxe handles.'

'That's true,' said Pelling.

'The trouble is,' said Wool, 'a colonel: what training has he got for civvy street? I mean, I was a driver. I remustered from infantry. I could find my way around an engine, too, at one time. Nowadays, of course, least little thing and she goes back into the garage. The firm pay all the repair bills. But coming out a sergeant with my mechanical skill made me a more desirable employee than you.'

'Very likely,' said Pelling.

'After all, you were just pointing at maps and giving orders. We were the people who actually did the work.'

'That's true.'

'It is true, isn't it? See, and in peacetime your good wages goes to chaps who do the real work.' He heaved himself round in his seat and from a large carton in the rear seat he brought a Munchy bar and unwrapped it.

'Like us?' supplied Pelling.

Failing to find irony in Pelling's impassive face, Wool broke the Munchy into four large pieces and offered the open wrapper to Pelling, who declined. Pelling knew that there would be cold meat and pickles waiting on the sideboard. Vaguely, he wondered what was on TV.

'Ever go back to Italy?' Wool asked.

'Never,' said Pelling.

'Don't like the Eyeties, eh? Yeah, I understand. I went back a couple of times. Package tour, very nice. Six cities in eighteen days. Just enough time to see the sights, not long enough to get bored. Course, I like the Eyetie food,' he patted his stomach. 'Perhaps it's too oily for you, but I eat a lot of it: *fettuccine alla panna*, *osso buco*, *lasagne al forno*. I'm quite an expert on the old cuisine Italiano. Mind you, you have to watch them with the women, they've got no respect for womanhood. My eldest was pestered by some waiter-type in Florence, but I didn't have no nonsense. I reported him to the management and said I was a director of the firm that runs the tours – I'm not of course – and they sacked him.'

At least he went back, thought Pelling, he didn't start four letters and finish none of them.

Pelling said, 'So when you went out that night, you weren't primarily trying to get the wounded fellow – Keats – back to the farmhouse?'

'Your memory,' said Wool. He chuckled. 'It must be even worse than mine. No, the Lieutenant was right.

16

That MG 42 had sliced old Keats up good and proper. The way I saw it, they probably had him in their sights, waiting for some medal-hungry twit to walk into them. I didn't want to go near him.'

For the first time Pelling was clearly able to recall the young Corporal who had been with them that day and night. But everthing about Wool had changed: his build, face, voice and demeanour. The corporal had been a wiry fellow with a shy smile, a red face and a thin London accent. Wool finished his Munchy, burped, loosened his belt and reached for a jacket hanging behind him.

'Look at this, Colonel.' He delved into his wallet, pulling out paper money and various business cards and stuffing them back with tuts of irritation until he found what he was looking for: a photo. 'That's what I've done for myself. I may not have been an officer but that's what I've done for myself.'

Pelling expected a photo of wife and family, but it was a photo of a house. Close behind it there were many others. 'Nineteen thousand,' said Wool. 'Probably worth twenty-five by now. My old Gran left me her little house in the country. But it was a dead-and-alive little hole, so I sold it for nine hundred and had enough to put down on a bungalow in Morden. Do you know South London at all?'

'No.'

'It's a very nice place where we live: doctors and that live there, well-to-do people. It's so convenient to London, you see.' While he was talking he'd sorted through his wallet and found another photo. He showed it to Pelling. Six young men, tanned and smiling, stood arms linked in the blazing African sun.

'You were a different fellow then,' said Pelling.

'I was a little twit,' said Wool bitterly, as though he hated the man that he saw in the photo. 'Yes sir no sir three bags full sir. Creeping around, apologizing for being alive.'

'That's not how I remember you,' said Pelling. 'You were full of life, laughing and joking. And you were full of ideas too.'

'Was I?' said Wool. He could not remember the terrain or the tactical situation in the way that the thirty-year-old Pelling had remembered. Wool's memories were simpler: the cold corned beef that he didn't eat; Keats, the squint-eyed little Scottish private with the wrist-watch he'd taken from a dead German Grenadier; and the posh Lieutenant who pronounced Tedeschi so perfectly that Wool had imitated it ever since.

It made no difference which of them was assigned to guard duty, for they all sprawled on the floor near the windows. They ate their cold rations where they sat and passed their cigarettes from hand to hand, leaving their positions only to use the latrine pit twenty paces across the back yard.

'That's wealth, that farmland,' said a private soldier named Stephens. He jerked his head towards the smashed window. Before the war he had been a solicitor's clerk and was duly respected as educated.

'D'ye not see these Italian farmers with the arse out of their trousers. Do you ken that, Stevie?'

'Land is wealth,' repeated Stephens, 'but not necessarily a sound investment.'

'Get on!' said Private Teasdale. 'Look at the price of a titchy little bottle of olives. About one and threepence, and how many in it? Bleeding twenty!'

'A dozen, more like,' said Stephens, relieved to move the conversation away from the subject of land, of which he had only a tentative understanding. He stole a glance at the olive plantations on big tit. The hillside was studded

18

with them and Stephens abandoned the task of calculating how many olives might be there.

'What about gold?' said Private Keats. 'Bugger owning a farm! Too much like bloody hard work. What I'd want is a neat little gold mine. Dig up a couple of ounces every week. Just enough to pay the rent and give the old lady something to back her fancy at the dogs. That's real wealth, gold is.'

'Wealth is energy,' said Stephens. 'You know: power stations, hydroelectric stuff, plant and factories . . . even muscle power. Wealth is just energy.'

'If you ask me,' said Corporal Wool, speaking for the first time in several minutes, 'wealth is time.'

'What you mean, Corp?' said Andrews. The new Corporal had that afternoon helped Andrews bring the water in from the Sapper Colonel's Jeep without anyone asking him to. You didn't get many corporals like that, in Andrews's experience. This one should be cultivated. 'Time is wealth, like?'

'It's the only thing you can't buy, apart from good health,' said Wool. 'I mean, we think we've got the worst end of the stick, being up here at the sharp end being shot at, right?' The others nodded. 'But you think any of those old generals and that back at Div wouldn't change places, no hesitation?'

'Would they?' said Keats. It was a thrilling concept. One to be toyed with. He hoped that it wouldn't be exploded too soon.

'Course they would,' said Wool. 'Here we are, fit and well and raring to go, with all our life in front of us. Course they would. Why, any of us could do anything . . .'

'Well, not exactly anything,' modified Stephens, who felt his position as the educated man might be jeopardized by the Corporal.

'Anybloodything,' said Wool. 'Any of us could become generals or millionaires or bloody film bloody stars with the right gumption and a bit of luck.'

'Get away,' said Keats scornfully, but not so scornfully as to disturb the dream. Rather he said it to coax more details from the pink-faced Corporal. This fellow could do it, thought Keats. He might become a general or a millionaire or a film star. Or even a centre-forward for Celtic, which was Keats's personal daydream.

'I tell you,' said Wool, 'time is all you need. Twenty-odd years from now we could all be whatever we decide on.'

'I'd like to be a centre-forward for Celtic,' said Keats, believing that an early claim would have more chance of fruition.

Teasdale said, 'I'd like to have a little grocer's in Nottingham, near the tobacco factory. Lots of married women work there, they have to buy the food for the old man's supper on the way home. In the side street for preference, and stay open late on pay night. And sell fags and sweets, too.'

Stephens said, 'I'd have studied to be a solicitor, but I'm too old now.'

'You're not,' said Wool, 'honest, Stevie, you're not too old. That's what I'm telling you. It's time that's wealth. When this lot's over you'll have time to be a solicitor. You could end up a judge, even.'

'And what about you, Corp?' said Andrews.

'Oh, me,' said Wool. 'I'm lucky in a way. I've got my future all waiting for me. My old Gran in the country has got five acres. I'll get a cow and some pigs and chickens. I won't make a fortune but I won't be worrying my guts out trying to make a living either. You become a different sort of person in the country. Everyone does, it's more natural somehow.' It was then that Wool raised his eyes

20

for a periodic glance at the horizon. 'Two Ted Mark IVs turning off the track, near the road at two o'clock.'

Wool's voice alarmed Pelling, just as it had done at the time. 'You were a cool customer,' said Pelling. 'I'll tell you frankly, I was afraid when that shell hit the loft, but you climbed up there before any of us had recovered our wits. It was some silly joke you made that brought us all back to normal again. And then there was the tank . . .'

'I was a twit,' said Wool, pushing the memory of the loft and its smell of warm blood back into his dark subconscious. 'Full of crap about esprit de corps, comradeship and loyalty. I'm not like that now, I'll tell you.'

'What are you like now?' asked Pelling flatly.

'I'm a go-getter. I look after number one and make sure that my expense sheets are countersigned and submitted bloody early. There's no esprit de corps in the chocolate-bar business.'

'I shouldn't have let you go out to the tank,' said Pelling.

'How could you have stopped me? I knew it was my last chance before your bloody sappers arrived.'

'You knew I was going to demolish the tank and the cowshed?'

'I didn't know anything about a cowshed, but I knew the salvage crew for Cindy Four had been taken off the roster. It was easy to guess what that meant for Cindy.'

'Why did you go out to the farm then?'

My bloody knee, that's the second time. It's damned dark! This field must be full of Conner cans, and the remains of the corned beef stinks to high heaven. God, what a smell. Why was he here, that was a good question. He had no orders to be risking his neck, in fact he had no permission to be absent from the laager. If he copped it tonight – and the chances were that he would – he'd be posted as a deserter and neither his Mum nor his Gran would get the money. Stop. Still, absolutely still. Ugh! What had he touched: crap? No, it's all right. It's only Keats. A swarm of bloated flies buzzed around his face. Angrily he waved them away and, so dozy were they, his hand hit some of them in mid-flight. Poor Keats with half his head missing, you poor old sod. I would have let you play for Celtic, Keats. I would have given half my Gran's fields to have you play once for Celtic, with me in front of the stand, eh? With a funny hat and rattle. Just that afternoon Keats had said, 'You know, Corp, you've changed my bleeding life in a way. You're right, I mean anybody can do bleeding anything, Corp.'

Careful; stinging nettles, and beyond them the ditch. Lucky that there's no moon. The night was cloudless; he could see every star for a million miles, except where a piece of night sky without stars was the Sherman tank. Another pile of cans. Just one tin-can makes a noise like a peal of bells on a night as quiet as this. He froze quite still. He could hear his blood pulsing.

At his Gran's the net curtains were floor length. At night the wind made them billow and arch as if a thousand phantoms were climbing through the window, one behind the other. But these were no ghosts. No ghost for Keats, no ghost for any of them.

Bloody hell!

There were voices whispering. Whispering sounds the same in all languages, but that won't be any of our boys standing out here in the dark on the German side of that Sherman. He put his hand upon the tracks; it was tight and true this side. One foot went on to rubber tyre and the other on to the suspension. Silently he eased open the turret hatch and put one foot down on to the breech of the gun . . .

'No, no, no,' said Pelling. 'You can't get away with that rubbish. Talk about hiding *under* a tank and I might

22

believe you, but climbing into a tank to avoid being seen is like climbing Nelson's Column to avoid being arrested. Anyway, I timed you that night. You'd only been gone eight minutes before the tank engine started. We were scared stiff, we thought the Mark IVs were returning.'

'You don't climb into a tank,' Wool corrected primly, 'you mount it. She started first go. Of course, I knew she would. I bet Sergeant Anderson she would. Five bob. He knew I wouldn't tell a lie about it. Paid up as nice as ninepence when I came back.' Wool reached behind him for another chocolate bar. Pelling didn't want any, but Wool bit into it greedily. 'Can't keep off them,' he explained waving the bar in the air. 'Mind you, they are damned good; butter, eggs and four ounces of full-cream milk in every one. The kids love . . .'

'Where did you learn to drive a tank?'

'Haven't you been following me, Colonel? I was the tank driver.'

'*The* tank driver?'

'Of Cindy Four. That was mine, that tank. I came out to get her back in, didn't I?'

'Tank salvage team?'

'Tank salvage team,' Wool repeated in scathing mockery. 'Those stupid bleeders. Those knacker's-yard attendants. I was a real tank driver. I was Cindy Four's driver.'

'You'd come out to get your tank without permission?' Pelling's incredulity as a Colonel was tempered by his understanding as an engineer.

'My skipper – Sergeant Anderson – knew, he was covering for me. The rest of the crew knew too. They all wanted to come at first, but me alone was best.'

'But it was a thousand to one she wouldn't have started. The tank had been there four days.'

'A thousand to one,' scoffed Wool. His voice was

scornful, as sometimes Pelling's had been when questioned by those who were mechanically illiterate. 'I knew Cindy Four like I know my old woman. Better. Better than my old woman.'

He pushed the rest of the Munchy into his mouth. 'I told that berk Lieutenant Kirkbride that I was the only driver who understood her. But no, he must have his own driver: that little twit Abbott, it was. They had to abandon: gearbox jam. Pausing, that was all you had to understand. Especially coming down from fifth into first. I told him never to use first, she'd start away fine in second even on a mountainside. But he has to use first. They were in a bit of soft-going, a ditch near the water trough. A good driver watches out for that sort of thing and doesn't get stuck in the first place. Pausing . . . you know.'

'Yes, I know.'

'I could have strangled bloody Kirkbride when I heard. And Abbott. But luckily for them they'd copped it already. Machine-guns got all four of them. Course, I was pleased they'd got themselves out. I'd have never been able to lift four bodies out and get her going.'

'I think you might have done almost anything that night.'

'Yeah,' grinned Wool. 'I suppose I would have done, but not in eight minutes.'

'You did all that, just for your vehicle?' asked Pelling. It was comforting to know that there were other maniacs. Men who would risk their lives to save that of a machine.

'This wasn't a *vehicle*,' explained Wool, repeating the word with studied distaste. 'This was a Sherman Firefly. Perhaps you don't understand what she was. Five 6-cylinder Chevrolet engines on a common crankshaft and a 17-pound gun. Nothing could stop it, nothing.'

'But the German Mark IVs were still at the end of the track. They could have brewed you up, from that close.'

'Wilson – our gunner – thought of that. He told me to elevate and traverse the 17-pounder so that the Teds would get an eyeful of it against the skyline.'

'But you were alone. You couldn't have loaded, fired and driven the tank, all by yourself . . .' But already Pelling wasn't so sure.

'No need. If I'd been in those Mark IVs I would have scarpered, too. Tank men understand that. You don't hang around to get brewed. Our 17-pounder was ace of trumps. They buggered off, didn't they?'

'They must have thought it was an ambush,' said Pelling.

'They didn't know what to bloody think. I had them doing their nut. I fired my revolver, all six rounds, at both of them. I knew that they'd hear that OK and that's all the commanders would need to keep their swedes under cover. When you are closed down you can't see bugger-all. Only tank crews understand how bloody help-less you feel with the lid on. You're always convinced that there's some sod of an infantryman farting about under your elbow with a bazooka. That's all it needs to brew you, whether you're in a Panther or a pantechnicon.'

'I never realized that the visibility was so poor,' said Pelling.

'Good God, yes. And then there were those bloody ditches. I never saw any of those in the south, but as soon as we reached that bloody ditch country I'd do anything to avoid driving down even a long straight road in daylight unless we had the hatches up and the old Andie shouting left and right. It's no picnic, I tell you.'

'But you were hit.'

'Yeah, funny that. Only time, too. That bugger in the

second Mark IV let me have a 75-mm armour-piercing over his shoulder as he went over the ridge.'

'We heard it strike the armour.'

Wool chuckled. 'I'll bet you did; so did I. Made my head sing for a week and took a quarter of a hundred-weight of metal off the side of the turret. Gouged it out as neat as a chisel mark.'

'We thought you were a goner.'

'The whole inside of the tank lit up bright yellow. I could see my controls and the gears and stuff, brighter than I'd ever seen it before! Then it went orange and glowed red hot at the point of impact before it all went dark again. I thought I was going to brew. The old Sherman had a terrible reputation for brewing. Ronsons, they called them; automatic lighters, see?'

'Didn't they ask you about the damaged turret when you got the tank back to leaguer?'

'You say leaguer, do you. My mob always said laager. No. Well, yes, they did, but I kept my mouth shut. I didn't want any trouble about it. They guessed it was me that brought it back, of course, but nothing was ever said.'

'They must have thought it was an ambush, Mr Steeple.'

'But who the devil's driving it, sir?'

'It must have been that little Corporal of yours, Steeple. The one who never stops smiling.'

'He's not one of my chaps, sir. I thought he was with you.'

'Deserves a medal, whoever he is. I'd get your chaps together and pull back until first light, Steeple. You can't defend this place with half a dozen Lee Enfields and a Bren. We can congratulate ourselves upon not going into the bag this night.'

'Indeed, sir, or worse.'

Pelling's voice was flat. 'Or worse. Quite so.' Was it fatigue that made him daydream so readily?

Thirty years ago it was, when I came closest to meeting my maker. Father Franco nodded, he'd heard the story before, as Father James well knew, but Compline was done and the evening still light. Here in the shadowy corner of the great hall the stories that he told seemed from another world. And yet Father James was not the only cleric who had been a professional soldier, and the things of which he spoke had taken place not many miles away from where the cliff-like monastery caught the harsh sunshine and tolled the hours of ceaseless prayer.

'I'd have put you in for an MM, Wool, but I had no idea of who you were.'

Wool was not impressed. 'It's all good and nice, you saying that now. I never got a medal, and what good would it do me anyway? Frankly, I'm more interested in Munchy outlets.'

'You saved twenty or more lives that night. Drove off an armoured attack, single handed. There's not many men who can say that.'

Wool was scarcely listening. 'She was a lovely bus, Cindy Four. Lucky tank, too. All four of us went through fifteen months without a scratch. Bert Floyd – the leader originally – copped it three days after being recrewed. It was only the gearbox that ever gave trouble and I could handle that. I knew the smell of her: lovely. That night as I strapped tight into the seat and grabbed the sticks I could smell the leather and the oil that the sun had warmed during the day. The Betty Grable pin-up was still next to the visor, and so was the red-painted ammo box from Sicily where Andy kept his bottled beer and a pair of carpet slippers.' Wool laughed. 'If we'd ever had to abandon, Andy would have been dancing about a battlefield in slippers. And when she started – beautiful!

'It broke my heart when they re-equipped us with Comets. I took Cindy back to the depot myself. I got special permission from the CO. He said they were going for training, but the RSM at the depot said they were to be sold for scrap. If I'd have had the money I'd have bought her. We tried to have a whip round but none of us had enough to even start. A bloody rotten shame,' said Wool bitterly, 'those Chevvy five by sixes were every bit as good as the V-8 jobs.' He plucked Pelling's sleeve and whispered, 'I had to do for her myself.'

'I beg your pardon?'

'At the depot,' said Wool. 'I poured sand into her and pushed her up to full revs. She stalled, horrible. I'd brought the sand in my small pack. The boys all agreed with me. No one could get on with that gearbox except me, and Wilson's turret had a lot of funny little ways that no one else would have understood.'

'I wish I'd seen her,' said Pelling quietly.

'To you she would have looked just like any other Sherman.'

'Oh, no,' protested Pelling. 'I understand what . . .'

'You, you, you . . .' spluttered Wool, 'you thought she was a Churchill. It was you went there to blow her up!'

'I didn't know,' said Pelling.

'I couldn't get you a job,' said Wool. He sniffed loudly and wiped the back of his hand across his eyes. 'So don't build your hopes on me.'

There was no more to say. Wool started the car even before Pelling scrambled out. He accelerated so that the gravel rattled against the pumps and he swung out of the forecourt on to the main road with an agonized squeal of tyres.

Pelling waved, but Wool didn't look back. He watched the car as it grew smaller upon the long straight road south.

Winter's Morning

Major Richard Winter was a tall man with hard black eyes, a large nose and close-cropped hair. He hated getting out of bed, especially when assigned to dawn patrols on a cold morning. As he always said – and by now the whole Officer's Mess could chant it in unison – 'If there must be dawn patrols in winter, let there be no Winter in the dawn patrols.'

Winter believed that if they stopped flying them, the enemy would also stop. In 1914, the front-line soldiers of both armies had decided to live and let live for a few weeks. So now, during the coldest weather, some squadrons had allowed the dawn patrol to become a token couple of scouts hurrying over the frosty wire of no-man's-land after breakfast. The warm spirit of humanity that Christmas 1914 conjured had given way to the cold reality of self-preservation. Those wiser squadrons kept the major offensive patrol until last light, when the sun was mellow and the air less turbulent. At St Antoine Farm airfield, however, dawn patrol was still a gruelling obligation that none could escape.

'Oatmeal, toast, eggs and sausages, sir.' Like everyone else in the Mess tent – except Winter – the waiter spoke in a soft whisper that befitted the small hours. Winter preferred his normal booming voice. 'Just coffee,' he said.'But hot, really hot.'

'Very good, Major Winter, sir.'

The wind blew with enough force to make the canvas flap and roar, as though at any moment the whole tent would blow away. From outside they heard the sound of tent pegs being hammered more firmly into the hard chalky soil.

A young Lieutenant sitting opposite offered his cigarette case, but Winter waved it aside in favour of a dented tin from which he took cheap dark tobacco and a paper to fashion a misshapen cigarette. The young officer did not light one of his own in the hope that he would be invited to share in this ritual. But Winter lit up, blew the noxious smoke across the table, coughed twice and pushed the tin back into his pocket.

Each time someone entered through the flap there was a clatter of canvas and ropes and a gust of cold air, but Winter looked in vain for a triangle of grey sky. The only light came from six acetylene lamps that were placed along the breakfast table. The pump of one of them was faulty; its light was dull and it left a smell of mould on the air. The other lamps hissed loudly and their eerie greenish light shone upon the Mess silver, folded linen and empty plates. The table had been set the previous night for the regular squadron breakfast at 8 A.M., and the Mess servants were anxious that these three early-duty pilots shouldn't disarrange it too much.

Everyone stiffened as they heard the clang of the engine cylinder and con rod that hung outside for use as a gas warning. Winter laughed when Ginger, the tallest pilot on the squadron, emerged from the darkness rubbing his head and scowling in pain. Ginger walked over to the ancient piano and pulled back the edge of the tarpaulin that protected it from damp. He played a silly melody with one finger.

'Hot coffee, sir.' The waiter emphasized the word 'hot', and the liquid spluttered as it poured over the metal spout. Winter clamped his cold hands round the pot like a drowning man clinging to flotsam. He twisted his head to see Ginger's watch. Six twenty-five. What a time to be having breakfast: it was still night.

Winter yawned and wrapped his ankle-length fur coat round his legs. New pilots thought that his fur overcoat had earned him his nickname of 'the Bear', but that had come months before the coat.

The others kept a few seats between themselves and Winter. They spoke only when he addressed them, and then answered only in brief formalities.

'You flying with me, Lieutenant?'

The young ex-cavalry officer looked around the table. Ginger was munching his bread and jam, and gave no sign of having heard.

'Yes, sir,' said the young man.

'How many hours?'

Always the same question. Everyone here was graded solely by flying time, though few cared whether the hours had been spent stunting, fighting or just hiding in the clouds. 'Twenty-eight and a half, solo, sir.'

'Twenty-eight *and a half*,' nodded Winter. 'Twenty-eight *and a half! Solo!* Did you hear that, Lieutenant?' The question was addressed to Ginger, who was paying unusually close attention to the sugar bowl. Winter turned back to the new young pilot. 'You'd better watch yourself.'

Winter divided new pilots into assets and liabilities at either side of seventy hours. Assets sometimes became true friends and close comrades. Assets might even be told your misgivings. The demise of assets could spread grief through the whole Mess. This boy would be dead within a month, Winter decided. He looked at him: handsome, in the pallid, aristocratic manner of such youngsters. His tender skin was chapped by the rain and there were cold sores on his lip. His blond hair was too long for Winter's taste, and his eyebrows girlish. This

31

boy's kit had never known a quartermaster's shelf. It had come from an expensive tailor: a cavalry tunic fashionably nipped at the waist, tight trousers and boots as supple as velvet. The ensemble was supplemented by accessories from the big department stores. His cigarette case was the sort that, it was advertised, could stop a bullet.

The young man returned Richard Winter's close examination with interest. So this rude fellow, so proud of his chauffeur's fur coat, was the famous Bear Winter who had twenty-nine enemy aircraft to his credit. He was a blotchy-faced devil, with bloodshot eyes and a fierce twitching eyebrow that he sometimes rubbed self-consciously, as if he knew that it undid his carefully contrived aplomb. The youngster wondered whether he would end up looking like this: dirty shirt, long finger-nails, unshaven jaw and a cauliflower-knobbly head, shaved razor-close to avoid lice. Except for his quick eyes and occasional wry smile Winter looked like the archetypal Prussian *Schweinhund*.

Major Richard Winter had been flying in action for nearly two years without a leave. He was a natural pilot who'd flown every type of plane the makers could provide, and some enemy planes too. He could dismantle and assemble an engine as well as any squadron fitter, and as a precaution against jams he personally supervised the loading of every bullet he would use. Why must he be so rude to young pilots who hero-worshipped him, and would follow him to hell itself? And yet that too was part of the legend.

The young officer swallowed. 'May I ask, sir, where you bought your magnificent fur coat?'

Winter gulped the rest of his coffee and got to his feet as he heard the first of the scout's engines start. 'Came off a mug I shot down in September,' he bellowed. 'It's from a fashionable shop, I'm told. Never travelled much myself, except here to France.' Winter poked his fingers through four holes in the front. Did the boy go a shade paler, or had he imagined it in the glare of the gas lights? 'Don't let some smart bastard get your overcoat, sonny.'

'No, sir,' said the boy. Behind him Ginger grinned. The Bear was behaving true to form. Ginger dug his knife into a tin of butter he'd scrounged from the kitchen and then offered it to the cavalry officer. The boy sniffed the tin doubtfully. It smelled rancid but he scraped a little on to his bread and swamped it with jam to hide the taste.

'This your first patrol?' asked Ginger.

'No, sir. Yesterday one of the chaps took me as far as Cambrai to see the lie of the land. Before that I did a few hours around the aerodrome here. These scouts are new to me.'

'Did you see anything at Cambrai yesterday?'

'Anti-aircraft gunfire.'

Winter interrupted. 'Let's see if we can't do better than that for you today, sonny.' He leaned close to the boy and asked in his most winning voice, 'Think you could down a couple before lunch?'

The boy didn't answer. Winter winked at Ginger and buttoned his fur coat. The other motors had started, so Winter shouted, 'That's it, sonny. Don't try to be a hero. Don't try to be an ace in the first week you're out here. Just keep under my stinking armpit. Just keep close. Close, you understand? Bloody damn close.' Winter flicked his cigarette end on to the canvas floor of the tent and put his heel on it. He coughed and growled, 'Hurry up,' although he could see that the others were waiting for him.

From the far side of the wind-swept tarmac, Major Winter's Sergeant fitter saw a flash of greenish light as the Mess tent flap opened and the duty pilots emerged.

Winter came towards him out of the darkness, walking slowly because of his thick woollen underwear and thigh-length fleece boots. His hands were tucked into his sleeves for warmth, and his head was sunk into the high collar that stood up around his ears like a cowl. Exactly like a monk, thought the Sergeant, not for the first time. Perhaps Winter cultivated this resemblance. He'd outlived all the pilots who had been here when he arrived, to become as high in rank as scout pilots ever became. Yet his moody introspective manner and his off-hand attitude to high and low had prevented him from becoming the commanding officer. So Winter remained a taciturn misanthrope, without any close companions, except for Ginger who had the same skills of survival and responded equally coldly to overtures of friendship from younger pilots.

The Sergeant fitter – Pops – had been here even longer than the Bear. He'd always looked after his aeroplane, right from his first patrol when Winter was the same sort of noisy friendly fool as the kid doing his first patrol this morning. Aeroplanes, he should have said: the Bear had written off seven of them. Pops spat as the fumes from the engine collected in his lungs. It was a bad business, watching these kids vanish one by one. Last year it had been considered lucky to touch Pops's bald head before take-off. For twelve months the fitter had refused leave, knowing that the pilots were truly anxious about their joke. But Pops's bald head had proved as fallible as all the other talismans. One after another the faces had been replaced by similar faces until they were all the same pink-faced smiling boy.

Pops spat again, then cut the motor and climbed out of the cockpit. The other planes were also silent. From the main road came the noise of an army convoy hurrying to get to its destination before daylight made it vulnerable to attack. Any moment now artillery observers would be climbing into the balloons that enabled them to see far across no-man's-land.

'Good morning, Major.'

'Morning, Pops.'

'The old firm, eh, sir?'

'Yes, you, me and Ginger,' said Winter, laughing in a way that he'd not done in the Mess tent. 'Sometimes I think we are fighting this war all on our own, Pops.'

'We are,' chuckled Pops. This was the way the Bear used to laugh. 'The rest of them are just part-timers, sir.'

'I'm afraid they are, Pops,' said Winter. He climbed stiffly into the cramped cockpit and pulled the fur coat round him. There was hardly enough room to move his elbows and the tiny seat creaked under his weight. The instruments were simple: compass, altimeter, speed-ometer and rev counter. The workmanship was crude and the finish was hasty, like a toy car put together by a bungling father. 'Switches off,' said Pops. Winter looked at the brass switches and then pressed them as if not sure of his vision. 'Switches off,' he said.

'Fuel on,' said Pops.

'Fuel on.'

'Suck in.'

'Suck in.'

Pops cuddled the polished wooden prop blade to his ear. It was cold against his face. He walked it round to prime the cylinders. That was the thing Pops liked about Winter: when he said off, you knew it was off. Pops waited while Winter pulled on his close-fitting flying helmet; its fur trimmed a tonsure of leather that had faded to the colour of flesh.

'Contact.'

'Contact.' Pops stretched high into the dark night and brought the blade down with a graceful sweep of his hands. Like brass and percussion responding to a conductor, the engine began its performance with a blinding sheet of yellow flame and a drum roll. Winter throttled back, slowing the drum and changing the shape and colour of the flame to a gaseous feather of blue that danced around the exhaust pipes and made his face swell and contract as the shadows exploded and died. Winter held a blue flickering hand above his head. He felt the wheels lurch forward as the chocks were removed and he dabbed at the rudder bar so that he could see around the aircraft's nose. There was no brake or pitch adjustment and Winter let her gather speed while keeping the tail skid tight down upon the ground.

They took off in a vic three, bumping across frozen ruts in the balding field with only the glare of the exhausts to light their going. It was easy for Winter; as formation leader he relied on the others to watch his engine and formate on him accordingly. At full screaming throttle they climbed over the trees at the south end of the airfield. A gusty crosswind hit them. Winter banked a wing-tip dangerously close to the tree tops rather than slew into the boy's line of flight. Ginger did the same to avoid his Major. The boy, unused to these heavy operational machines with high-compression engines, found his aircraft almost wrenched from his grasp. He yawed across the trees, a hundred yards from the others, before he put her nose up to regain his position in formation. Close, he must keep close. Winter spared him only a brief glance over the shoulder between searching the sombre sky for the minuscule dots of other aeroplanes. For by now the back lid of night had tilted and an orange wedge prised open the eastern horizon. Winter led the way to the front lines, the others tight against his tailplane.

The first light of the sun revealed a land covered by a

grey eiderdown of mist, except where a loose thread of river matched the silver of the sky. Over the front line they turned south. Winter glanced eastwards, where the undersides of some low clouds were leaking dribbles of gold paint on to the earth. As the world awakened stoves were lit and villages were marked by dirty smoke that trailed southwards.

Major Winter noted the north wind and glanced back to see Ginger's aeroplane catch the first light of the sun as it bent far enough over the horizon to reach them at fifteen thousand feet above the earth. The propeller blades made a perfect circle of yellow gauze, through which reflections from the polished metal cowling winked and wavered as the aeroplanes rose and sank gently on the clear morning air.

Here, on the Arras section of the front, the German and French lines could be clearly seen as careless scrawls in the livid chalk. Near the River Scarpe at Feuchy, Winter saw a constant flicker of artillery shells exploding: 'the morning hate'. Pinheads of pink, only just visible through the mist. Counter-battery fire he guessed, from its concentration some way behind the lines.

He pulled his fur collar as high round his face as it could go, then raised his goggles. The icy wind made his eyes water, but not before he had scanned the entire horizon and banked enough to see below him. He pulled the goggles down again. It was more comfortable, but they acted like blinkers. Already ice had formed in the crevices of his eyes and he felt its pin-pricks like daggers. His nose was numb and he let go of the stick to massage it.

The cavalry officer – Willy, they called him – was staring anxiously at the other two aeroplanes. He probably thought that the banking search was a wing-rocking signal that the enemy was sighted. They read too many cheap magazines, these kids; but then so had Winter before his first posting out here: 'Ace of the Black Cross', 'Flying Dare-Devils', 'True War Stories'.

Well, now Winter knew true war stories. When old men decided to barter young men for pride and profit, the transaction was called war. It was another Richard Winter who had come to war. An eighteen-year-old child with a scrapbook of cuttings about Blériot and the Wright brothers, a roomful of models which his mother wasn't permitted to dust and thirteen hours of dangerous experiments on contraptions that were bigger, but no more airworthy, than his dusty models. That Richard Winter was long since dead. Gone was the gangling boy whose only regret about the war was leaving his mongrel dog. Winter smiled as he remembered remonstrating with some pilots who were using fluffy yellow chicks for target practice on the pistol range. That was before he'd seen men burned alive, or, worse, men half-burned alive.

He waved to frightened little Willy who was desperately trying to fly skilfully enough to hold formation on his bad-tempered flight commander. Poor little swine. Two dots almost ahead of them to the south-east. Far below. Ginger had seen them already but the boy wouldn't notice them until they were almost bumping into him. All the new kids were like that. It's not a matter of eyesight, it's a matter of knowledge. Just as a tracker on a safari knows that a wide golden blob in the shadow of a tree at midday is going to be a pride of lions resting after a meal, so in the morning an upright golden blob in the middle of a plain is a cheetah waiting to make a kill. So at five thousand feet, that near the lines, with shellfire visible, they were going to be enemy two-seaters on artillery observation duty. First he must be sure that there wasn't a flight of scouts in ambush above them. He looked at the cumulus and decided that it was too far from the two-seaters to be dangerous. Brownish-black smoke patches appeared around the planes as the anti-aircraft guns went into action.

Winter raised his goggles. Already they had begun to mist up because of the perspiration generated by his excitement. He waggled his wings and began to lose height. He headed east to come round behind them from out of the sun. Ginger loosed off a short burst of fire to be sure his guns were not frozen. Winter and the boy did the same. The altitude had rendered him too deaf to hear it as more than a ticking, as of an anxious pulse.

Winter took another careful look around. Flashes of artillery shells were bursting on the ground just ahead of the enemy planes' track. The ground was still awash with the blue gloom, although here and there hillocks and trees were crisply golden in the harsh oblique light of morning. The hedges and buildings threw absurdly long shadows, and a church steeple was bright yellow. Winter now saw that there were four more two-seaters about a mile away. They were beginning to turn.

Winter put down his nose and glanced in his mirror to be sure the others were close behind. The airspeed indicator showed well over a hundred miles an hour and was still rising. The air stream sang across the taut wires with a contented musical note. He held the two aeroplanes steady on his nose, giving the stick and rudder only the lightest of touches as the speed increased their sensitivity.

Five hundred yards: these two still hadn't seen their attackers. The silly bastards were hanging over the side anxious not to get their map references wrong. Four hundred.

The boy saw them much later than Ginger and Winter. He stared in wonder at these foreign aeronauts. At a time when only a handful of madmen had ever tried this truly magical science, and when every flight was a pioneering experiment to discover more about this new world, he hated the idea of killing fellow enthusiasts. He would much rather have exchanged anecdotes and information with them.

Ginger and Winter had no such thoughts. Their minds were delivered to their subconscious. They were checking instruments, cocking guns and judging ever-changing altitudes, range and deflection.

If that stupid kid fires too early . . . damn him, damn him! Oh, well. Ginger and Winter opened fire too. Damn, a real ace gets in close, close, close. They'd both learned that, if nothing else. Stupid boy! The artobs leader pulled back on the stick and turned so steeply as almost to collide with the two-seater to his left. He knew what he was doing; he was determined to make himself a maximum-deflection shot. Winter kept his guns going all the way through the turn. The tracer bullets seemed unnaturally bright because his eyes had become accustomed to the morning's gloom. Like glow-worms they were eating the enemy's tailplane. This is what decided a dogfight: vertical turns, tighter and tighter still. Control-stick held into the belly, with toes and eyes alert so that the aeroplane doesn't slide an inch out of a turn that glued him to the horizon. It was sheer flying skill. The sun – a watery blob of gold – seemed to drop through his mainplane and on to his engine. Winter could feel the rate of turn by the hardness of his seat. He pulled even harder on the stick to make the tracers crawl along the fuselage. The smell from his guns was acrid and the thin smoke and heat from the blurring breechblocks caused his target to wobble like a jelly. First the observer was hit, then the pilot, throwing up their hands like badly made marionettes. The two-seater stalled, falling suddenly like a dead leaf. Winter rolled. Two more aeroplanes slid across his sights. He pushed his stick forward to follow the damaged two-seater down. Hearing bullets close to his head, he saw the fabric of his upper plane prodded to tatters by invisible fingers which continued their destruction to the point of breaking a centre section strut and throwing its splinters into his face. His reflexes took over and he went into a vertical turn tighter than any two-seater could manage. Aeroplanes were everywhere. Bright-green and blue wings and black crosses passed across his sights, along with roundels and dark-green fabric. One of them caught the light of the sun and its wings flashed with brilliant blue. All the time Winter kept an eye upon his rear-view mirror. A two-seater nosed down towards his tail, but Winter avoided him effortlessly. Ginger came under him, thumping his machineguns with one of the hammers which they all kept in their cockpits. He was red-faced with exertion as he tried to clear the stoppage by force. At this height every movement was exhausting. Ginger wiped his face with the back of his gauntlet and his goggles came unclipped and blew away in the air stream.

Winter had glimpsed Ginger for only a fraction of a second but he'd seen enough to tell him the whole story. If it was a split round he'd never unjam it. Trees flashed under him. The combat had brought them lower and lower, as it always did.

The new boy was half a mile away and climbing. Winter knew it was his job to look after the kid but he'd not leave Ginger with a jammed gun. A plane rushed past before he had a chance to fire. Winter saw one of the two-seaters behind Ginger. My God, they were tough, these fellows. You'd think they'd be away, with their tails between their legs. Hold on, Ginger, here I come. Dive, climb, roll; a perfect Immelmann turn. The world upside

41

down; above him the dark earth, below him the dawn sky like a rasher of streaky bacon. Hold that. He centred the stick, keeping the enemy's huge mainplane centred in his sight. Fire. The guns shook the whole airframe and made a foul stink. He kicked the rudder and slid down past the enemy's tail with no more than six feet to spare. A white-faced observer was frozen in fear. Up. Up. Up. Winter leaned out of his cockpit to see below him. The new boy is in trouble. One of the two-seaters is pasting him. The poor kid is trying for the cloud bank but that's half a mile away. Never throttle back in combat, you fool. White smoke? Radiator steam? No, worse: vaporizing petrol from a punctured tank of fractured lead. If it touches a hot pipe he'll go up like a torch. You should have kept close, sonny. What did I tell you. What do I always tell them. Winter flick-rolled and turned to cover Ginger's tail.

Woof: a flamer. The boy: will he jump or burn? The whole world was made up of jumpers or burners. There were no parachutes for pilots yet, so either way a man died. The machine was breaking up. Burning pieces of fuel-soaked wreckage fell away. It would be difficult to invent a more efficient bonfire. Take thin strips of timber, nail them into a framework, stretch fabric over it and paint it with highly inflammable dope. Into the middle of this build a metal tank for 30 gallons of high-grade fuel. Move air across it at 50 mph. Winter couldn't decide whether the boy had jumped. A pity, the chaps in the Mess always wanted to know that, even though few could bear to ask.

The dogfight had scattered the aeroplanes in every direction, but Ginger was just below him and a two-seater was approaching from the south. Ginger waved. His gun was working. Winter side-slipped down behind a two-seater and gave it a burst of fire. The gunner was

42

probably dead, for no return fire came and the gun rocked uselessly on its mounting. The pilot turned steeply on full throttle and kept going in an effort to come round in a vertical turn to Winter's rear. But Ginger was waiting for that. They'd been through this many times. Ginger fired as the two-seater was half way through the turn, raking it from engine to tail. The whole aeroplane lurched drunkenly, and then the port mainplane snapped, its main spar eaten through by Ginger's bullets. As it fell, nose-down, the wings folded back along the fuselage like an umbrella being closed. The shapeless mess of broken struts and tangled steel wire fell vertically to earth, weighted by its heavy engine which was still roaring at full throttle. It was so low that it hit the ground within seconds.

Winter throttled back and came round in a gentle turn to see the wreckage: not a movement. It was just a heap of junk in a field. Ginger was circling it, too. From his height the sky was a vast bowl as smooth and shiny as Ming. They both looked round it but the other two-seaters had gone. There were no planes in sight. Winter increased his throttle and came alongside Ginger. He pushed his goggles up. Ginger was laughing. The artillery fire had stopped, or perhaps its explosions were lost in the mist. They turned for home, scampering across the trees and hedges like two schoolboys.

Winter and Ginger came over the airfield in echelon. Eight aeroplanes were lined up outside the canvas hangars that lacked only bunting to be a circus. A dozen officers fell over themselves scrambling out of the Mess tent. One of them waved. Winter's machine, painted bright green with wasp-like white bands, was easily recognized. Winter circled the field while Ginger landed. He'd literally lived in this French field for almost a year and knew each tree, ditch and bump. He'd seen it from every possible angle.

43

He remembered praying for a sight of it with a dead motor and a bootful of blood. Also how he'd focused on blurred blades of its cold dewy grass, following a long night unconscious after a squadron booze-up. He'd vomited, excreted, crashed and fornicated on this field. He couldn't imagine being anywhere else.

For the first time in a month the sun shone, but it gave no warmth. As he switched off his engine the petrol fumes made the trees bend and dance on the heavy vapour. Pops hurried across to him but couldn't resist a quick inspection of the tail before saluting.

'Everything in order, Herr Major?'

Winter was still a little deaf but he guessed what the Sergeant was saying. He always said the same thing. 'Yes, Sergeant. The strut is damaged but apart from that it probably just needs a few patches.'

Winter unclipped his goggles, unwound his scarf and took off his leather helmet. The cordite deposits from his Spandaus had made a black band across his nose and cheeks.

'Another Englishman?' said Pops. He warmed his hands before the big Mercedes engine, which was groaning softly.

'Bristols: one forced down, one destroyed. We lost the new young officer, though.' Winter was ashamed that he didn't know the boy's name, but there were so many of them. He knew he was right to remain unfriendly to all of them. Given half a chance new kids would treat him like some sort of divinity, and that made him feel like hell when they went west.

Winter wiped the protective grease from his face. He was calm. Briefly he watched his own unshaking hand with a nod of satisfaction. He knew himself to be a nerveless and relentless killer, and like any professional assassin he took pride in seeing a victim die. Only such men could become aces.

First Base

'The first time I ever heard that word I'd just reached Junior High.'

'What word?'

'Vietnam.'

'That's a real dirty word for a kid in Junior High.' Dutch laughed and deliberately steered the truck into a giant puddle that glinted on the road. There was a roar as the water pounded against the floor of the cab.

'Take it easy, Dutch. I once saw one of these six by sixes slew into the Mekong off a wet road and he wasn't doing more than forty.'

'Shoot. I was handling artics when I was fifteen.'

'That don't mean that you can't skid an army truck.'

'So how did you hear it in Junior High?'

'My teacher was drafted.'

'Well, I bet the termites got that mother since way back.'

'The fighting was way up north somewhere: Inchon. He came back in a casket: flowers, speech by the mayor, picture in the papers, pallbearers, bugler playing taps and an Honour Guard fired volleys over the grave. Us kids got a day out from school. That's fifteen years since.'

'It's going to be a long war, Des, old buddy.'

The young soldier smiled. He was a slim blond boy, only just twenty-one. His complexion was pale and on one pink forearm there was tattooed the word 'Mother'. He'd won fifteen bucks for having it done one night in San Diego – the night before shipping out here. He'd been drunk. He'd like to get it removed before he saw his family again. Before being drafted, Des Jones had been in the packing department of a shirt factory in Mohap, Massachusetts, where his parents and their parents also lived. Des had no plans for his future except to get out of Vietnam, get out the army and go back to Mohap, where he would marry some unspecified virgin and buy a split-level home with oil-fired heat and a pool.

The driver – Dutch Relay – was a plump Negro from Detroit. He'd been a truck-driver in Detroit and continued to be a truck-driver in the army. He couldn't remember a time when he wasn't a truck-driver: he'd dropped out of school when he was twelve. Dutch was twenty-four years old; unshaven, dirty and prematurely wrinkled, he could have been mistaken for forty. However, his build and weight made up for his poor physical condition, as could be testified by a PFC in Da Nang who spoke out of turn to Dutch and was hospitalized to the land of the big PX, as the soldiers refered to the US. Dutch had often wondered who got the best of that exchange of blows.

They didn't look like soldiers. Their fatigues were ill fitting and dirty and their movements slow and casual. They did not have the quickness of eye that shooting gave, nor the precision of men who had stood sentry. Even their skin had the softness of sedentary civilians, for a benign army had contrived to manufacture for its servicemen conditions of life that corresponded as closely as possible to life at home. In some cases it was better.

Even the truck was equipped with mechanical refinements of a sophisticated sort: power braking and steering and fully adjustable seats. On the seat between them there was a transistor radio. Dutch used one hand to search the wavebands for a programme to his taste. Finally he found the US Armed Forces channel. It was playing Country and Western music. Dutch turned the volume very loud and joined in the vocal. It was difficult to reconcile his short-syllabled urban grunts with the yodelled vowels of the show-biz cowboy on the air.

For almost half an hour they drove along the highway, Dutch singing tunelessly and Des Jones of Mohap, Massachusetts, watching the heavy tropical rain fighting the high-speed wipers and roaring down the irrigation ditches alongside the road like a miniature tidal wave. The first time he'd ever seen this country on the map it had looked a tiny place, not much bigger than his home state. He'd expected its roads to be lined with native villages like he'd seen in movies, where slim bare-breasted girls danced and chubby kids sold mangoes and sun-ripened melons for a nickel apiece. The reality was different. You could roll a hundred miles down this highway and seldom catch sight of a human face, except for pale GI smudges that peered out of trucks coming the other way. And the green, lush tropical countryside that he'd imagined was buried under grey dust most of the year, except when the monsoons churned it into bottomless mud. Sometimes he'd catch a glimpse of what used to be a native village: trees cleared back from the road, broken pieces of timber leaning against the few remaining uprights and sheets of corrugated iron flapping in the wind.

Sometimes he wondered exactly what had happened to the people in those villages. Some of the lucky ones had been evacuated, the rest had been killed or had fled. Sometimes the infantrymen that he'd drunk with back in the depot at Da Nang had told him horror stories about the fighting. Some boasted of the villages that they'd shot up or fired, but Des didn't always believe the loudmouths who came looking for an audience among the supply men.

He shifted in his seat and put his paratroop boots up on the dash. His leg was getting cramp. A month ago they used to stop on the road near here. It was very hot then, and they had sat in the cab with the doors open and drunk beer and eaten cold chicken from the Mess. Now that the rains had started they did the journey without stopping. Without even lowering the window a quarter of an inch lest the fever-stinking rain soaked them both.

Dutch reached behind the sun visor and felt for the box of cigars that was tucked behind *Stars & Stripes*. He lighted it himself and smoked in silence. He didn't offer Des one; they were so cheap in the PX that it was understood that he'd ask if he wanted. He'd only taken a few puffs at the evil-smelling stogie when he dabbed the brakes. They screamed and puffed as the huge truck and its heavy trailer slowed to thirty. The wheels bumped over some pot-holes with enough violence to make both men hammer their heads against the head rests. He hit the brakes again, more violently this time.

'Whoa,' shouted Dutch standing on the brakes. They stopped.

'Je . . . sus,' said Des. He'd wound the window fully down, and oblivious of the torrents of rain he leaned out of the cab and peered ahead into the grey afternoon gloom. The low black clouds were moving fast across the ragged trees that whipped and roared with a noise like gunfire. The road zigzagged: about eighty yards of the grey army-laid highway had slipped neatly into the jungle on the left. At each end the errant section was held by only a few threads of wire mesh underlay. Even as they watched, more chunks from the broken part collapsed into the irrigation ditch and pounded away into the dark jungle.

Both soldiers got out of the truck, careless of the driving rain.

'You think the VC have mined her?'

'No, mister,' said Dutch. 'Either they would have

48

blown the surface more completely than that or they would have waited until we were rolling over her.'

'Maybe they figured to hijack our load.' Des looked back to the truck. Its sidelights flickered in the rain, distorting the drops into little spears of yellow water as they passed the lamps. He could still hear the transistor radio playing Country and Western.

'Vietcong got no use for filing cabinets, man.'

'Is that what we're carrying?'

'Don't you ever read the manifest?'

'Sometimes.'

'Well, I always do. If it's something like jackets or food or electric stuff I count her twice. 'Cos those thieving bastards who onload that stuff can make a crate disappear like suds down a gulley. Those studs are the ones you see down in Saigon riding the tinted-glass Caddies with half a dozen go-go girls in the back and a general driving. Those guys can move towns, buddy boy, never mind crates.'

'Our load's OK ?'

'With Corporal Relay, no sweat, soldier. In fact we made one extra crate of flashlight batteries.'

'You goddamned gold brick!'

'The Polish Mafia, son – that Sergeant Bzin treats me like I'm his long-lost son.'

'But you're not Polish,' said Desmond.

The Negro opened his eyes wide and puffed his cheeks in mock fear. 'But you ain't going to tell him, are you, Des?'

Desmond punched him playfully. 'I might at that. What are we going to do, Dutch?'

'Do – Dessy boy? We're going to shift arse back on to Route 15 and hit the Delta country from the west.'

'You know the way?'

'Bet your life. This section of highway walked into the

jungle last year – no, make that six months ago – I found the way that time.'

'Can you turn her – trailer and all?'

'Goose me when I'm on the verge, Des.'

Dutch climbed into the cab and gunned the motor. It was a tricky feat of driving, to U-turn the long truck and its equally long trailer on that narrow highway. Dutch could probably have done it, if the edges of the road hadn't crumbled under the load when the trailer wheels were still three feet from the irrigation ditch.

'She's going, Dutch,' screamed Des. The weight of the combination pulled the truck back, in spite of the four-wheeled drive and the skilful way in which Dutch used the accelerator. Still she moved, sliding against the brakes. When the back wheels of the trailer hit the bottom of the ditch the movement stopped, while the torrent of rainwater made a new path that incorporated the twin offside wheels and a part of the power-lift mechanism on the tail.

Dutch got out and cussed quietly.

'We'll never get her out now,' said Des.

'Tell me something I don't know, soldier.'

'Unhitch?'

'Unhitch.'

'Suppose the VC come back and take the load away?'

'So we stay here and the VC take us away, too. Is that better?'

'No.'

'So unhitch.'

It was even hotter on the road than it had been in the cab, where they had two five-dollar fans going all the while. By the time they had unhitched the trailer they were not only soaking with warm smelly rain but literally smeared with oil and grease. And they were up to the

50

ankles in gluey brown mud that almost sucked their boots off.

'Now let's go,' said Dutch. Des Jones stared into the bottom of the irrigation canal. As the dirty water swirled round the deep treads there was still enough daylight to read the word 'Dunlop' on the casing. And to see two arms and an army boot poking out of the gurgling stream.

'I think there are two guys here, Dutch.'

'Is that right?' said the plump driver. He was pulling the front wheels past the overhanging roots of a tree and trying to avoid the other ditch. Dutch would have appreciated some help. 'Dead GIs,' called Desmond.

'Must have been some kind of war here,' said Dutch.

'But, Dutch . . .'

'Jump in, kid . . . and move it, unless you want to hike back.'

He ran to the cab and jumped in. They sped back north along the road they'd come. 'I wondered why the oncoming traffic had gone dry.'

'Dutch, what about those bodies? Maybe they were cops sent there to flag us down.'

'Same thought occurred to me, buddy boy.' He pressed the accelerator pedal to get more distance between them and the incident. The transistor radio was still playing loudly. Desmond turned the volume down. 'What you do that for, Dessy?'

'I can think better when it's quiet.'

'So can I, Dessy,' agreed Dutch and turned the volume up again.

'How much longer you got, Dutch?' said Des. His voice was thin. He cleared his throat with a loud cough.

'Ninety-three days. You?'

'Over six months. You think we'll ever lick the Commies?'

'Who knows?' said Dutch.

51

'What do you think it would be like: Communism?'

'Communism is like being in the army for ever, man,' said Dutch.

'I suppose,' agreed Des. 'In this war, Dutch, we are the Redcoats.'

'How's that?'

'We're the Redcoats and the VC are the settlers. I mean, you've got to hand it to the VC: they'll tackle a tank with a slingshot. Half their weapons are built from junk. They've got the know-how and we've become stuffy like the British. It's the world turned upside down.'

'Well, next time you see a squint-eyed little Paul Revere – yell real loud, man!'

Dutch had no doubt about the turn-off. There was a ruined building that had once been a café or a shop or something. Behind it were half a dozen rusting motor-car bodies. This road was narrower than the major highway they'd been on so Dutch was a little relieved that he'd lost the trailer. He was mentally composing the accident report that he would file. They went about thirty miles due west before getting to a crossroads with a battered yellow signpost SERIES G REPLACEMENT BATTALION with an ornate badge and a list of the units that were there.

Dutch heaved a sigh of relief and turned to follow the arrow. They went about three miles up that road, the trees converging more and more until it was little better than a track.

'They've got to be kidding,' said Dutch.

'The sign must have been wrong.'

'It meant straight on,' agreed Dutch. He was so relieved about the chance to gas up and eat that he hardly swore at all at having to reverse the truck for three-quarters of a mile before finding a clearing. Even then they didn't take any chances about getting stuck. Dutch did a twenty-five-point turn, using only the very centre of the roadway.

'That's funny,' said Des.

'Ha bloody ha,' acknowledged Dutch when they had travelled five miles on the clock. They still had not seen the yellow sign.

'There was a fork.'

'There were three, but I would have sworn this was the way we came.'

'Haven't got a compass, have you, Des?'

'Nope, and there's not even a glint of sunlight to navigate by.'

'That's dandy, boy. That's real dandy.'

'We're lost?'

'Oh no – just don't know where we are, that's all.'

Dutch flicked the switch on the radio. There came a sudden burst of solo guitar before he twisted it off again. 'What do we do, Dutch? Sleep in the cab?'

'Looks like.'

'You think there could be Cong about here?'

'Cong is everywhere. Don't you know that yet?'

'Jesus, Dutch. Let's roll on until the gas gives out.'

'And wind up down some arse-hole alley like that one we had to back out of?'

'Roll on until the reserve light comes on.'

'You got a deal. Left or right?'

They had come to a T-junction. There were no signposts or people, and no huts, not even wrecked ones; just the rain-swept jungle growing darker by the minute.

'Right for guesses – but don't get mad.'

'Right it is, buddy boy.'

This road was wider than the previous one, and after only a few minutes they saw a sight that gladdened their hearts as few other things could have done. The verges had been cleared of large trees so that a fifteen-foot wire fence could be seen beyond the grass and mud. Every hundred yards there was a sentry tower and a long way

53

away – perhaps a mile or more – there was enough light left in the low cloud to shine upon the gleaming silver metal of three US Air Force transport planes. Even from as far away as this they looked impressive; inanimate representatives of another world as different to this mess of jungle as any man-made object could be. It was another half mile before they came upon an entrance gate to the compound and even then it was a small access gate to the airfield instead of the main gates.

'Welcome to Series G Replacement Battalion!' said Dutch. He laughed and switched on his radio again.

'You think that's what we're at?'

'Work it out for yourself. Three Boeings that have just delivered a cargo of Cong-fodder and are waiting to rotate some old and weary vets. Look!'

Through the driving rain they saw a big sign on the perimeter track: WELCOME TO VIETNAM. It was placed exactly where the transports would stop to unload soldiers, before taxiing on to the Maintenance Sheds on the far side of the complex. On the nearest building there were more signs – plentifully provided with crests and badges and enormous coloured arrows – R & R MEN REPORT HERE, ATC CREWS ONLY, FIREARMS PROHIBITED BEYOND THIS POINT, BAGGAGE CENTER D. There was the whole complex machinery of modern war, painted to look like a super-market special.

'Looks like we could just take off with the whole parade, Dutch.'

'Yeah,' said Dutch. His voice registered a new fear: perhaps he'd been a little hasty in abandoning several thousand dollars' worth of military supplies and a new trailer out on that jungle road. He was preparing some really frightening stuff for the top sergeant and embroidering Des's discovery of the dead soldiers into a heroic retreat under fire.

'Where in Christ is everyone?'

'Let's find out,' said Dutch. He stopped the truck outside a building marked EM MESS HALL. HAVE YOUR CHIT READY.

'We didn't see a living soul since pulling out.'

'They stopped the war, that's for why. They waited till we was on the road and then they shipped every mother-loving son of them Stateside. You and me, Dessy, are the only people still fighting.'

'Should we open negotiations for peace?' Des wanted to join in with Dutch's joke, but he didn't feel much like it. Even before they were halfway up the path of the Enlisted Men's Mess they knew what they'd find inside.

'Empty, good goddamn!'

They looked around the stoves and into the cupboards. They found five gross of plastic spoons and a dozen eggs. Des cracked one of the eggs – it was a big Stateside type of egg – and the smell chased them out of the kitchen. 'This place ain't been used in an age.'

'It's the pull-back. Who needs a dozen EM Messes any more. Let's go chase up another one. Failing that I breeze into the Officers' Club, right?'

'Right.'

Dutch took the road through the depot but most of the buildings were just warehouses for air freight. On the other side of the base road – Westmoreland Avenue – there were barrack huts. All of those were empty, too, their windows smashed and in some cases the roof caved in.

Dutch turned back up Main Street – the sight of that street sign made him feel better – as far as the control tower and then turned to drive along the taxi-way towards the transport planes. The wind across the airfield was so strong that it made the truck veer alarmingly. Dutch laughed grimly.

They were gigantic aircraft, half a city block in length with tailplanes several storeys high. Aeroplanes, big or small, have a characteristic smell. It's a compound aroma of canvas, battery acid, leather, hydraulic fluid, rubber and high-octane fuel. These aeroplanes didn't smell like that. These were dead aeroplanes, abandoned after Vietcong rockets had blasted their tailplanes. Air force engineers had taken away the jet motors so that the cowlings hung down and clattered in the wind like muffled drums.

The two soldiers went through the inside of the planes. The seats had been taken, and so had removable fittings like flashlights, radios and radar sets. They had both hoped that the inside of the plane would be comfortable, but the thin metal skin was icy and there were enough holes in it to let the wind through the cabins.

'Don't worry, kid, we'll find somewhere.'

'I sure hope so, Dutch. This place gives me the creeps.'

They went back to the truck and Dutch drove round the whole airfield. There was just a chance, he said, that there would be a small guard unit left here. Dutch was wrong; there was no living human anywhere. When they got to the west end of runway 90 Dutch turned off along the taxi-way to get straight back to Main Street. He touched the brakes a little too firmly and the truck began to slide.

'Easy does it, Dutch.'

But already the big fellow had corrected the skid and put her into a new skid just for the fun of it.

'Dutch! Dutch! Dutch!' Then Dutch saw it too. Appearing out of the rain was a tanker, abandoned on the runway and robbed of wheels. Des could only hold on to the frame of the cab and stare in horror at the ghostly truck that seemed to steer away from them for a moment before the explosion.

It made a frightening sound: a tin belly gutted by the

sharp steel chassis of the six by six. After a resounding clang as the tank collapsed, there was the gulp of liquid and the sound of it splashing upon metal and concrete. Only then did the heavy vapour rise into the warm night air, billowing over red hot metal in varying densities until one of them was exactly right. Only then did the air explode.

If Des had done what the drill said, he wouldn't have been stunned for a moment and thrown out on to the hard concrete. Then perhaps he would have been able to wrench Dutch from inside the burning tanker quickly enough for his burns to be only superficial.

'Oh Jesus, Jesus, Mother of God.' Dutch was whimpering and calling softly. He was hunched up on his side; Des was afraid to pull his hands away to look at his injuries. 'I'm bad, Des, help me, kid. I'm real bad, hurt real bad, Jesus.'

The flames were bright enough to light up the whole runway. Any minute now, thought Des, there'll be some GIs running to see what they can do. The thought gave him momentary relief until he remembered that any VC in the district would also see the burning trucks. And all we needed was gas, thought the boy; with a tankerful we could have driven to hell and back. It took him five minutes to untie the tarpaulin from a pile of packing cases. All the time he was praying for a sharp knife. When he got it clear he put it on the wet runway and rolled the groaning Corporal on to it. He wrapped it right over him, as one would prepare a corpse for burial, then he took the ropes through the eyelet holes near Dutch's head and tugged him across the wet ground.

'Sorry, Dutch,' he said.

Dutch thought that the boy meant to abandon him and said, 'Don't leave me, Des. In God's name don't leave me.'

57

Desmond was unable to distinguish the separate words; to him it sounded like a prayer. He dragged him right across the tarmac saying, 'I'm sorry,' when the jolts seemed particularly bad. Dutch Relay, who'd had most of his life's pain muted by alcohol, suffered more than ever before. It washed over him in waves and manifested itself in coloured sheets of bright light that exploded behind his eyelids and told him what sort of pain was going to surge through his body. Red blobby pains were dull numbing ones but thin streaks of yellow made tears well in his eyes and brought him cruelly close to the unconscious state he sought.

It was almost dark by now. The horizon was flickering with bluish-white flashes. It might have been an electrical storm or rocket fire; there was no way of telling. In this war there was no front line – just people trying to kill you. When he'd dragged Dutch as far as the first building, Desmond had to roll him over the step outside the door. The door was bolted but it was made of some compressed paper compound. He broke a hole through it, reached for the latch and let himself in.

The lobby was decorated with blue-velvet wallpaper dotted with large gold-paper stars. To the right there was a hat-check counter and a rail that still had a dozen wire hangers on it. Over the double doors ahead of him was a large mural depicting a man in evening clothes and a girl in sequins, against a background, painted in exaggerated perspective, of men in white tuxedos playing distorted saxophones. In neat lettering above them it said OFFICERS' CLUB.

Desmond got Dutch on to a chesterfield too badly broken to have been worth transporting, and wheeled it to the most sheltered part of the TV room. Then he used up a box of matches examining Dutch's burns. None of them were really deep, and some were only blisters that

58

had not punctured the skin, but they covered such a large percentage of his body that Dutch was in an advanced state of shock and dehydration. 'Find me some water.'

'You be all right, Dutch?'

'Just don't take off altogether, Des. Will you promise?'

'What on, Dutch? We ain't even got a roller skate, remember?'

'That's right.' He forced a smile. He was reassured now by the lack of transport.

'What time you got?'

'Eight twenty.'

Des adjusted his watch. 'OK. I'll be back by nine, right?'

'You're a good kid.'

The first thing that Des Jones did was look all around the Officers' Club. He decided he'd never get the chance to see inside such a place again, which in the event proved right. Then he walked out into the rain. The heavy rainstorm had passed over. Now there were just a few light raindrops hitting the puddles and making the moon split in two and shake like a jelly. He didn't go back into the EM Mess. They'd looked thoroughly around that. He used a piece of iron fencing to break the locks off one of the warehouses. The doors were almost too heavy for him to roll but he waited a few minutes to collect his breath and finally managed to get them back with a noise like thunder.

It was dark inside. The warehouse was as large as an aeroplane hangar, and the only moonlight came from tiny clerestory windows high in the walls near the curved roof. It was dry in here. Underfoot the concrete floor was dusty, and he heard the scuffle of rats that for a moment frightened him into taking cover behind a crate. He'd been a truck-driver long enough to read the code stencils:

portable field toilets, freezer wrap in rolls, dishwasher detergent, Tabasco sauce, Akai tape recorders. ·

PX supplies. Gee, he'd always wanted an Akai tape recorder. For a moment he was tempted to try to force that crate open, but he remembered Dutch and moved on. At this end of the warehouse some of the crates had already been forced open. He guessed that the storeman had looted the crates at the closed end of the warehouse, trusting to a careless check of the other end. There were some large tins that looked like orange juice, but upon closer inspection he found that the 'orange' on the label was a shiny table, and that the tins contained floor-wax. He sorted through the broken crates and found LPs of Tom Jones and Ray Charles. He took those with him and again looked back at the crate of Akai tape machines.

Dutch was getting a bit twitchy by the time Des got back to the Officers' Club at ten past nine, and was delighted to see him.

'Find anything?'

'Nothing to drink, Dutch. Tabasco sauce is all. But great PX stuff: radios . . . you name it.'

'Look around here, kid, find me a drink.'

Out in the lobby Desmond found two soft-drink cabinets. He was going to break the back off one of them and then he remembered that he had a quarter with him. He put it in the slot and pulled the handle. A warm bottle of Coke came down the chute. There was his change too. Des laughed and bought another. It was reassuring that the machine worked.

The two soldiers drank their Cokes and Des went back for more. With renewed energy he prepared them for the night. He ripped the plastic covering off the banquette with a broken Coke bottle and they wrapped themselves in the plastic stuffing. It wasn't warm, but it gave them the feeling of being covered and protected which they so badly wanted. They did not sleep very well and at first light, after another Coke, Des went on a proper journey of exploration. Given the daylight and hunger he broke into the second warehouse at record speed. He found tins of tomato paste and ate half of one. Then he found packets of blueberry muffin mix. He jettisoned the flour envelope and opened the tiny tin of blueberries. Nothing had ever tasted so good. There was macaroni cheese and chicken-and-dumplings in tins. Thousands of them. They didn't taste at all bad straight out of the cans, unheated. He took some back for Dutch. But Dutch's response was disappointing; he scarcely said thanks. Dutch had gone very silent and his open wounds smelled awful. Des hated to go near him.

That afternoon Des found the portable TV sets. The dry batteries were in a separate crate and he broke into six before he found which one. Some of the PX crates had a different coding to army supplies, to confuse looters.

Even Dutch liked the TV. That was the day that he seemed to be recovering. They could only get the Armed Forces TV channel, but it was miraculous to have someone talking to them in accents they knew. There was a girl disc-jockey who knew more about some of those Country and Western groups than their agents did. Desmond wondered what it would be like to have a girlfriend who knew everything about Country and Western.

On the second day Desmond found the emergency generator in the Operations Block. It was a Japanese one, but it was still in good condition and it gave enough power to work the lights and the freezer. Desmond looked at the silent figure of Dutch on the broken chesterfield and wondered what to do about him. He'd been sick, and the vomit had left patches over the front of his jacket. Desmond had put a bucket near him but Dutch had not been able to use it. There was a smell of excrement even in the far side of the room, where Des had put his armchair. 'They can't even help themselves,' he remembered his aunt saying. From her apartment in Chicago you could see the ramshackle tenements of a black ghetto in Sloan Street. His aunt always kept that window tightly closed because of the smell. Now that Dutch was losing interest in the TV, Desmond began to be more impatient with him. He couldn't understand why Dutch didn't thank him for getting the TV and the hi-fi and a heater going. Dutch said nothing, but he was a constant reproach to Desmond and a criticism of everything that Desmond had done, just as Sloan Street spoiled all the fun of his visits to Chicago.

The third day – when Des found the eight-track stereo in the departure lounge and played all the Guthrie records – was the day that Dutch died. He had fallen silent and wasn't much company for Des. Anyway, by that time Des had become as keen on the girl disc-jockey – Kathie Wayne Morris – as Dutch had been. The girl on the screen replaced Dutch as company for the boy. Once one of the batteries ran down during her 'À La Country-Style Hour'. Des was furious and afraid. To prevent that happening again he dragged forty batteries over to the Officers' Club on a piece of hardboard that had WELCOME BOB HOPE and a picture of Santa Claus painted on it. Santa Claus made a headstone for Dutch. Des dragged the body over to the office of the commanding officer and buried him in the patch of mud outside the window. Once it had been a flowerbed.

Private Desmond Jones may still be living there. There were enough tins of macaroni cheese and chicken-and-dumplings and enough dry batteries to last him for six years. Of course, it's dangerous to wander around outside, but you could say the same thing about his aunt's apartment in Chicago. And she hasn't got stereo hi-fi and twenty thousand brand-new LP records.

Paper Casualty

It was a still day. The grey stone house was lifeless, like a prehistoric shrine in some long-forgotten jungle. The lower windows were shuttered, but the upper ones reflected the bleached sky, their grimy panes glinting dully like fake diamonds in a pawned tiara. The hard tennis court was covered in nettles. On the terrace forget-me-nots hovered like mist, and dead daffodils, now only shrunken vellum relics of their blooms, were infiltrated by bluebells. The wood was dark. There, fern stalks curled liked poised vipers and disguised as soft green lace prepared to strangle the nettles in a fight for the patches of sunlight that stabbed through the trees.

Beyond the drive, this anarchy ceased. Flag plants grew out of the mud like bright green sabres, each bloom a polished brass hilt. Uniform in size, shape and colour, and spaced like guardsmen, they marked the place where in winter the river broke its banks. Today the water raced noisily over drowned trees and the collapsed embankment's stones. A young man, dressed in an old jacket and corduroy trousers tied at the knees, picked his way carefully along the overgrown path beside the water. A sow grunted loudly enough to alarm him, but he smiled as she turned and forced a noisy way through the undergrowth. He distrubed other creatures: pigeons that chortled loudly, and game birds that broke cover almost under his feet with a mighty rattle of anxious wings.

He went through the wrought-iron gate that marked the end of a short avenue of cedars. Beyond it, amid a chaos of roses, a collapsed portico, dock, nettles and daisies, there was a small heap of kindling. As he walked towards it his boots hit the pearly globes of dandelion so that he left a trail of seeds suspended in the air behind his feet. He picked up an armful of twigs, selecting the driest ones and including a few thick pieces. From here there was a fine view of the house and the landscape behind it. The scene was timeless, until an aeroplane passed over at thirty thousand feet, leaving a condensation trail that soon went blobby in the high-altitude winds and then smudged twenty miles across Kent before it disappeared. The man kept a watch upon the curve of the front drive; that was the way they would come. He went to a derelict outhouse and lit the stove there. From time to time he consulted a gold wrist-watch which he kept in his trousers pocket.

There were several false alarms. The sow wandered back that way and made as much noise coming through the bushes as a recruit infantry platoon. When the soldiers finally arrived they were two Corporals, each on a BSA motor-cycle. The senior wore a scarf across his face. He unwound it as he walked over to the civilian.

'Empty, eh?'

'That's right.'

'How long?'

'A long time; five years, perhaps.'

'Bloody fool! How long since they retreated through here, I mean.'

'Very late last night. I heard tanks and motor-cycles about midnight.' The Corporal nodded; that fitted with what his officer had told him. These two Corporals were 'point': the men at the very tip of an advancing army. Point discovered mines, traps, pill boxes and eventually the fortified positions at which a retreating army turned to fight again. Sometimes they didn't. Sometimes the defenders let the point pass by and saved their energies for the infantry and tanks, or even for the soft transport that came after. This dangerous duty left a mark upon the faces of men. One of them lit a cigarette and the other looked at his watch. They were early. They brought their motor-cycles up to the front terrace and rubbed the dirty glass of the porch, trying to see inside. The furniture was covered with white sheets and the carpets had been taken up. After ten minutes the two Corporals went away. They returned along the front drive as far as the road but they didn't follow the retreating enemy; they turned back north.

When the sound of tanks could be heard in the gardens of the house the civilian climbed the embankment behind the stables. From there he could see them; eight infantry tanks – Valentines, perhaps – were moving along the main road on the far side of Ten-Acre Field. It was difficult to identify them because of the leafy branches and netting that they wore. The commander of the lead tank was standing up in his turret talking into his microphone and looking ahead to where the two men on motor-cycles had by now disappeared. The other tanks were closed down for action.

The civilian descended from his vantage-point and went back to his stove. He searched for a cigarette and lit it carefully. This was the easiest way to infiltrate an army; let it advance right over you. It was an hour before any other soldiers came near the house. At 10.30 hours a 30-cwt lorry bumped up on to the little lawn adjacent to the gate house. Three soldiers climbed out, swearing. One of them lit a pressure stove to brew tea while the others changed the wheel. The civilian watched them from the end of the drive but they did not see him. Within twenty-five minutes they had finished, and accelerated away to catch up with their convoy.

At lunchtime a small Austin car came up the drive. It was painted khaki and had a Divisional sign, but was

clearly one of those vehicles that the army had comman-
deered. Two subalterns got out and hammered on the
door. The civilian shouted from the kitchen garden to tell
them that the house was empty. The two officers were
suspicious of him. They were all togged up in webbing,
steel helmets and pistols, and seemed uncertain whether
to hold the civilian at pistol-point. The man shrugged and
offered to show them through the house if they wanted to
see it.

He unlocked the oak door, and they kicked aside a
broken dog-basket and ancient advertisements that had
been put through the letter-box. The two officers kicked
the staircase, too, and jumped up and down upon the
wooden floor of the library to decide if it was sound.
They tried the taps in the kitchen and the scullery, and
got dirty searching the wine cellar.

It was the pink drawing-room that pleased the officers
most. When they drew back the heavy curtains the
sunlight came in like gold bars and made the mirrors
flash. The french windows came unstuck with a creak.
The dusty panes went white as they swung open and
revealed childish rude words scrawled on the glass. Those
walls would hold the maps, and the room was big enough
to hold the sort of briefing that the Divisional commander
wanted.

The Div HQ must already have been on the road, for
they began to arrive by three o'clock. There were lorries
and Jeeps and staff cars in such profusion that they had
to put a redcap on the terrace to arrange the parking.
The first-floor study became the map room, refreshments
were to be served in the dining-room, and the drawing-
room was filled with ten rows of stacking chairs ready for
the briefing.

The telephones were installed in the vinery because, by
breaking a glass pane, the signallers were able to pay out

66

cables to rear windows at all levels and put a field telephone on each sill. The soldiers did other damage; heavy lorries demolished part of the wall near the gate house by turning too sharply into the drive. Sappers cleared young trees and bushes from the near side of the pond so that the sentries could see all the meadow as far as the stream. The stables became a strong-point with a Bren in the loft, and they removed a few bricks to give it a traverse. A carrier left track marks right through the flowerbeds to the azaleas.

The interior of the house suffered, too. When they were fixing the maps a ladder cracked one of the ornamental mirrors, and two fine gilt chairs were broken by soldiers who stacked them carelessly in the basement kitchen. General Parkstone assigned an officer to record each damaged item and decide whether the culprit should be punished. Parkstone was not the sort of man who tolerated vandalism, even in a war.

When he arrived at the house, General Parkstone was asleep for the first time in forty hours. He was hunched across the back seat of his Humber with his cap tipped over his face and a book of poetry on the floor. His pale-blue eyes blinked awake as his driver opened the door. He recognized the cornices and the superb front door. He'd seen this house before. He'd seen almost every Georgian house in southern England. Prospect, this one was called, and Parkstone saw in that name the promise of a happy life as well as a fine vista. He felt a moment of envy for the man who'd designed and sited this mansion. He hurried inside where his batman had prepared a hot bath, clean clothes and a bowl of tinned soup.

This wasn't Parkstone's first war, as one glance at his greying hair and the ribbons on his chest confirmed. Before going to the Staff College in 1918 he'd won a DSO and Bar and an MC. Some said that the action at

Polygon Wood, when Parkstone brought in four casualties under fire and got a mention, would have got a VC for a lower rank. Not that Parkstone's past valour did him much good in his present job. Decorations from the First World War dated him. Beaten in France by a dynamic Panzer Army, the British had suddenly decided that youthful commanders were the secret of victory. 'Suspect,' a very senior officer had told Parkstone, tapping his medal ribbons, 'suspect, General!' Outraged by the injustice of such treatment, Parkstone had nodded. Even to remember it made him flush with shame.

For Major-General A. G. Parkstone was no blimp. A close friend of Swinton and Fuller, he'd been a tank man when such heresies were a great impediment to his career. Now that armoured warfare had become the epitome of fashion, Parkstone was accused of being the same sort of fogey that he'd spent his career opposing.

Lieutenant Fane came into the dining-room and checked the number of cups on the sideboard before opening a tin of biscuits that he had been jealously guarding for a week. He put them out on the plates, roughly calculating at three biscuits per officer. He was a tall elderly man with a bony nose and thin lips that he sometimes bit bloodless rather than lose his temper. Lieutenant Fane was Camp Commandant. He had spent most of his life as a senior NCO. In order to take charge of the domestic side of this Divisional HQ he'd got a commission, but he had no illusions about it. To the men around him he was still an NCO despite the salutes that he now got from his clerks and waiters, and Fane was satisfied that it should be so.

He looked around the room approvingly; his clerks had done a good job. It was almost impossible to believe that it had only been inhabited for a couple of hours. He'd found the carpets in the attic, and they were bright and clean as ever they'd been. He had chivvied the Catering Sergeant into lighting one of the kitchen stoves, and they'd found a collection of odd teacups and saucers in a tea-chest in the pantry. There was an army blanket over the dining-room table to protect it from careless cigarettes or hot teapots.

'A good effort, Camp,' said Parkstone.

'Sir!' Fane went to the door and placed a notice there: COMMANDING OFFICER'S CONFERENCE. NO ADMISSION. He nodded to the sentry. 'No one else.'

'Sir.'

The past inhabitants of the house would have rejoiced to see the dining-room that Tuesday afternoon in 1941. It had been as lively as this when young Victoria was crowned, and as sunny when Uncle Arthur celebrated his knighthood. There had been fireworks on the lawn at Mafeking, and an orchestra in the summerhouse for Emily's twenty-first. But never had the dining-room vibrated with the sound of so many polished masculine voices as when the senior officers of Parkstone's Division greeted their comrades, ragged their school chums and artfully probed the credentials of newcomers. They had all arrived by ten minutes to four, none of them wishing to face the cold greeting that Parkstone reserved for people who were merely punctual.

Major-General Parkstone, a slight, pale figure, circulated among his officers. Colonel Lee – who commanded one of the armoured regiments from inside his tank – was wearing clean, pressed overalls. Mitchell, Lee's Brigadier, was in shirtsleeve order, his khaki shirt bleached almost white. Chaps back from the desert liked to advertise the fact, thought Parkstone. He'd never got along well with Brigadier Mitchell, a blond thirty-seven-year-old with a tanned skin and a nose full of broken capillaries. Mitchell and his protégé Lee had both got mentions the previous

69

winter, when the 7th Armoured Division chased Bergan-
zoli and his Italians across Cyrenaica. Those two had
smelled the scent of victory, and breathed it proudly
among colleagues who had tasted the sand of Dunkirk.
Parkstone nodded to the two men and moved past them
to where his GSO1, Colonel Joyce, was standing near the
sideboard, examining a bowl of wax fruit inside its dusty
glass dome.

Joyce offered his commander a plate of biscuits. The
plump little Irishman, dark skinned from a quarter-
century of Indian sun, had still not got used to rooms and
streets full of white faces. He also had known victory, in
Africa, with his Punjabis. But defending the mountain
stronghold of Keren, the Italians had fought like tigers.
Joyce had watched his Indians die on every crag. He had
no illusions about blitzkriegs.

'Those oatmeal ones are grand.' Even after all the time
away, there were still traces of Kerry. The voice was
known to everyone in the room. Like every chief-of-staff,
he was able to manage on little or no sleep and spent
almost all his waking hours giving wireless orders. He'd
had only brief moments out of his command vehicle since
the battle had started.

Parkstone smiled and took a biscuit. Joyce was an old
friend. He, more than anyone, knew the difficulties he
faced. Armoured Divisions were the newest toys of the
General Staff. They only awarded them to their brightest
boys, that's why everyone wanted one. Some said it was
more difficult to get than a Corps.

'I'll take two, Joycey, while I've got the chance.' They
both smiled.

Lieutenant Fane appeared at the Irishman's elbow with
a glass of ice-cold beer. 'You're a darling man, Camp,'
said Joyce in a stage-Irish accent.

The old boy was a great organizer, thought Parkstone,

70

the best Camp Commandant he'd known. He did most of the Quartermaster's work, too. Parks nodded to Fane to tell him that they should soon be moving into the drawing-room. He wondered who the portraits could be: the girl in the pink dress, the two young country squires on horseback and the old man so proud of his knighthood that he'd had a scroll painted around his head like the halo on a martyr.

There was a noise that rattled the cut-glass chandelier as a formation of fighters came over the house at one thousand feet. Some of the officers moved to the french windows to catch sight of them before they disappeared over the tree tops.

'Spitfires,' said Mitchell.

'Off to the real war.' Colonel Lee brushed a biscuit crumb off his immaculate tankman's overalls.

'It won't be long now.' Mitchell smiled at his protégé. Unlike the others, they knew all about the real war. 'The Two Hussars', the others called them derisively but they liked this label; they relished its connotations of vigour and *élan*.

In the kitchen garden the young man also looked up at the Spitfires before glancing back at the senior officers moving past the hall window as they filed into the draw-ing-room. He'd tried to get around the terrace to glimpse the map on the wall, but there was an armed sentry on duty each side of the shrubbery, and even from here he could see that the drawing-room curtains were closed. He cursed his own stupidity in not hiding those curtains before the soldiers had arrived.

Major-General Parkstone lit a cigarette himself to avoid giving formal permission to smoke. It was dark in the curtained drawing-room, apart from the battery of lights that had been arranged to shine upon the blackboard and the map that were mounted on the platform.

'Two squadrons of armoured cars will be ahead as far as Maidstone. The infantry attached to the armoured brigade – that is to say, Sammy's battalion – will maintain contact with Brigadier Mitchell by means of the command tank. It is imperative that tank crews realize that the speed of advance will be dictated by the pace of the infantry. Infantry are the eyes of the advance; without them, closed-down tanks will get into trouble. I'll deal personally with any breach of this order.' Parkstone could see that the commander of one of the armoured regiments was fidgeting. 'Colonel Lee, you have a question?'

'Affirmative,' said Lee. He spoke in strange staccato bursts, like economical machine-gun fire. 'Maidstone: south of the river. Could give us a chance to break out. The recce squadrons give me the green light. I'd punch one of my sabre squadrons southwards and keep going.'

'The Guderian approach,' nodded Parkstone. It was strange that he had spent most of his life advocating breakthrough armour tactics without response. Then came Dunkirk, and now it had become necessary to curb everyone's desire to stage a blitzkrieg. 'This is not Sedan,' said Parkstone, 'we are not fighting the French . . .' he paused before adding, 'and you are not Guderian.' He gave the room a moment or two to absorb the reprimand he'd given Lee. 'If we put an armoured column down the Ashford road the enemy will tear open the flank of the whole Corps. Look.' Patiently Parkstone ran his hands across the map to explain the strategy of the battle from Portsmouth to Margate. Parkstone's Division was protecting London. Now that the Corps was advancing, Parkstone's task was to maintain contact with his flanks. Only that morning the Corps Commander had pointed out that Parkstone's front would be stretched by advancing. Strategically, the less he advanced the safer London would remain.

Outside, by the flowerbeds that skirted the croquet lawn, the man in civilian clothes made a decision. He had gathered a large bunch of mixed flowers and walked slowly towards the servants' entrance. Outhouses surrounded a cobbled yard on the east side of the house, and on a clothesline stretched across the yard hung khaki shirts and underclothes. Three batmen were sitting in the derelict dairy. They had got a fire going in an old stove near by and were drinking tea and chatting. The last of the row of outhouses had once been the head gardener's house, and an old sofa and some chairs were still there. The Military Police Sergeant had claimed it as his office. The man in civilian clothes pushed open the double gates to enter the courtyard and found himself half strangled by the Police Sergeant before he knew what was happening.

'And where are you off to, my pretty maid?'

'Flowers for the Officers' Mess dining-room,' grunted the man. The Police Sergeant did not relax his hold. 'Just drop them on the floor, chummy.' The flowers dropped to the cobbles and, still holding the man, the sergeant kicked them gently with his toe to be sure there was nothing concealed there. He released the man, who rubbed his neck and said, 'A nice mess you've made of the flowers now.'

'And a nice mess my General would have made of me if you'd gone waltzing into the house,' said the Police Sergeant. 'Who are you, anyway?'

'Pepper. I'm the gardener for Mr Matthews who owns Prospect. I'm the one that will get into trouble for all the damage your lot are doing.' He finished picking up the flowers. 'Am I allowed to take them inside now, or will you do it?'

The Police Sergeant patted Pepper's pockets and under his arms. Before the war he had been a prison warder, and he searched him with a swift professional flourish.

73

'OK Mr Pepper. Just as far as the kitchen door. Hand them to one of the cooks. I'll be watching you.' He glanced towards the house. The drawing-room was over the kitchen, but the curtains were still tightly closed.

'Just as you like,' said the man. When he got to the kitchen door he didn't knock, but took from his pocket four tin-tacks and a piece of red paper and fixed a notice to the door. The Police Sergeant ran to him, but the man in civilian clothes just stood and grinned. On the piece of paper was crudely printed the word 'Bomb'. In the bottom right-hand corner it was signed by a Captain Ridley on behalf of Lieutenant-General Post, the senior referee of the whole Southern Command Exercise.

'But good God Almighty,' said Parkstone, 'you can't kill a man with a sheet of paper.' He had the red paper in his hand and he kept examining it as though some new information might appear there.

'It's ridiculous,' agreed Colonel Joyce. 'I've been on to Command, but it seems our move this morning has rather outstripped the referees.'

'He was searched?' Parkstone asked for the fifth time.

'He was, sir, very thoroughly, by Sergeant Albany.'

'If he'd really had a bomb he would have found it.'

'Exactly, sir.'

'After all,' said Parkstone, forcing a smile, 'I could have sent the whole staff a postcard with "bullet" written on it. What then?'

Joyce nodded.

'You can't kill a roomful of chaps with a sheet of paper, Joycey, or the War Office would have obliterated the Jerries in the first week of war, eh?'

Joyce smiled.

'It's buggered the briefing.'

'Yes, sir, and I think you had them ready to go.'

'I think I did, Joycey.'

The General looked at his watch again. How long would this bloody referee be? Inevitably, his senior officers would be talking about this business. He wondered what they would be saying about it.

'Everyone thinks it's quite idiotic, sir.'

'Do you think we could find them all a real drink, Joycey?'

'If we used up your personal bar, sir. Then we could squeeze them out a small one.'

'Do that.'

The General sat down on his desk and sorted through his piles of paperwork: fire support, boundaries, water, fuel, daily objectives. But he couldn't take his mind off the paper bomb.

When the referee arrived it was Brigadier Frederick. Until Dunkirk, 'Bunny' Frederick had been noted for his immaculate appearance: Sam Browne, riding-boots, starched collars, the finest of gold-wire badges and a riding-crop in his formally gloved hands. Now, Parkstone noted sardonically, it was the age of the private soldier. Frederick was wearing an old battledress with a webbing belt and gaiters and a steel helmet with netting. His cloth badges had been carefully dirtied – to avoid snipers – and he'd exchanged his gold spectacles for a steel pattern frame that the army issued to recruits. He saluted.

'Hello, Bunny,' said General Parkstone.

'A fine how-do-you-do this is, Parks, old boy.'

'How do you want to do this, Bunny? Set up an office here and see this so-called spy and my Police Sergeant?'

'No needs, Parks. I know all the details, there's nothing to settle. The fellow has blown up your whole Div HQ. There's not one senior commander between Green Force and London. If they exploit the gap they'll be in London by tonight. Sorry old fellow.' The brigadier spoke rapidly

75

and tonelessly, like a child reciting a poem that it didn't understand.

'But Bunny, for Lord's sake listen. This chap was searched. All he had was a piece of paper – '

'Piece of paper to you, bomb to me.' He smiled. 'We're up against a tough opponent, Parks. The Hun is going to use every damned trick in the book and a few not in the book. Look at Holland: parachute troops dressed as nuns.' He slapped his thigh with an imaginary riding-crop.

'Must have been damned draughty up their skirts,' said Parks. 'I've never believed that stuff about paratroop nuns, a bit too much like some of those atrocity stories that came out of Belgium in the first lot.'

'Yes, well, you remember the first lot, of course. But this is a different sort of war we're fighting, Parks. You don't believe in nuns and you don't believe in spies – '

'I didn't say I don't believe in spies,' said General Parkstone. 'I don't believe in things that are not evidenced. I don't believe in paper bombs.'

'You underrate the enemy, sir,' said Bunny Frederick, 'if you don't mind me saying so.'

'I don't think I agree,' said Parkstone.

'Well, luckily it wasn't up to me. I went over to Army before coming here. That's what made me a bit late. The fact is, Parks, that the exercise will stop at 18.00 hours. It was agreed that there is no point in continuing with so many senior officers pulled out of the battle.' Frederick tugged at the brassard that had a large R on it. 'Five referees gave evidence and that was the decision. Sorry, Parks.'

'Did they say anything about me?'

Frederick shuffled, and pulled the strap of his respirator case so that it fitted more comfortably on his shoulder. 'The chief was in a black mood, Parks. They all were except Simms – you know, the G2 Major – it was his idea, the bomb. He was almost jubilant – expounding his theories about infiltration, you know.'

'I know.' Parks nodded. 'Think I'll lose the Division, Bunny?'

'Of course not, Parks.'

'You'd better tell me, Bunny. I'd sooner know from you.'

'It's only talk.'

'Say on.'

'It might go to Mitchell. The Chief wants young commanders. You can't blame him, Parks . . . the press, the PM, the politicians, all keep talking about Britain's new young army . . . recruiting jaw-jaw, don't you know.'

'A triumph for the Hussars.' He couldn't keep the bitterness out of his voice.

'Yes, Mitchell's lad Lee will probably get Mitchell's Brigade.'

Frederick walked across the room to look out of the window. He didn't want to look at Parkstone. He asked himself if he'd handled it terribly badly. He wished desperately that he had the deft touch of a diplomat, so that he could have lessened the blow. But Bunny Frederick wasn't a diplomat, or even a very good soldier. At Sandhurst where Under-Officer Parkstone was still something of a legend, Gentleman Cadet Bunny Frederick had been a dud, swotting like mad and sometimes cheating, just to end up with a pass into the army. His sympathy could be no comfort to a man like Parks. It would make him feel even worse; but at least Bunny Frederick knew this. 'Must have been a magnificent place once,' he said. 'You've always liked these Georgian country houses.'

'Detailing is a bit heavy,' said Parkstone mechanically,

'but the cornice is good and the front-door is pure Queen Anne.'

'Well, everyone knows you're an expert, Parks.'

Including Major Simms, thought Parkstone; he guessed I couldn't resist Prospect as a Div HQ. Parkstone had been in shirtsleeves, but now that the sun was behind the trees he felt cold. He put on his jacket and fastened the buttons carefully. It gave him a chance to think. Only half an hour ago he'd been sure that you can't kill a man with a sheet of paper; now he wasn't so sure.

Brent's Deus Ex Machina

Doctor John Garrard was a forty-year-old Flight Lieutenant, the Medical Officer at Brimington, a bomber airfield in East Anglia. He had done that job for nearly two years since 1940, when the bomber offensive was a puny, disorganized affair of a few dozen yougsters flying twin-engined Wellingtons and Hampdens. Now it was more impersonal, with fleets of four-motor bombers that dropped thousands of tons of bombs in one night; it was nothing to send five thousand airmen into the enemy sky on such nights. The flyers themselves had become less glamorous, less individualistic, more often drawn from the lower income groups and, as far Garrard was concerned, disappointingly inarticulate.

Nowhere was the difference more noticeable than in the privacy of Flight Lieutenant Garrard's consulting-room in Station Sick Quarters. The crews were blatantly self-important and had none of the respect for doctors that Garrard had learned to expect in general practice. The first time one of the new aircrew had admitted to him that he was frightened of continuing with operational flying, Garrard had been shocked speechless. Now it happened every couple of weeks.

Usually it was the gunners and flight engineers that came to him detailing the symptoms that rendered them unfit to fly in combat. 'It's not fair to the rest of my crew,' was what they usually told him. Their training was shorter than that of the other categories, their selection less stringent and their educational standards usually lower. Garrard often said that gunners and FEs had less

79

discipline, conscientiousness and integrity, and were apt to pay little attention to personal cleanliness. These were the ones that indulged in heroics, and felt free to put ground-staff officers – like Garrard – at a personal disadvantage by implying that they'd sought jobs that were safe. Garrard disliked gunners and engineers.

Officers were less likely to come to him pleading their inability to continue flying duties, and pilots were even rarer. But Brent was a pilot and an officer, and few patients declared their self-interest with his bland self-assurance. Doctor Garrard decided that Brent should never have been given a commission. He looked at the case history in Brent's medical file on the desk in front of him:

'Flying Officer Michael Peter Barnaby Brent, aged twenty-three, married. One child ten months old, one four. Pilot, total flying hours 115, of which 21 hours were operational. These hours were made up of three long bombing raids over Germany. From the third raid Brent's Lancaster returned slightly damaged by gunfire.

'On physical examination there was a slight tremor of the extended finger-tips and eyelids, but apart from a slight tachycardia his central nervous system and all other systems showed no sign of abnormality. His family history had no mention of neurotic traits and Brent himself seemed apprehensive only about a continuation of operational flying.

'Brent said he needed "a tonic" and some tablets to help him sleep. He said that when he was flying he suffered from "a blurring of the horizon" but a medical test showed no indication of this.

'During his last days at the Conversion Unit, where Brent was trained to fly the four-motor bombers, he landed heavily enough to break the ankle of his Flight Engineer (who alone of the crew stood upright during the

80

landing and take-off). No one else was hurt, although they were all taken into Sick Quarters and given the usual hot bath, meal, three grains of Nembutal and bed. Brent claimed that his blurred vision dated from this event.'

Doctor Garrard closed the medical file so that there was no chance of Brent reading it, then he walked to the window. He watched a bomber taxi around the perimeter track to the end of runway 27. From here he could see the flying control officer in the tower, and recognized him as Jammy Giles who had done two operational tours and won the DFC. Garrard stole a glance at Brent's reflection in the mirror. He'd placed it in the corner for this very purpose; it could be very revealing to watch a patient while he thought himself unobserved. Brent – he'd long since decided – was a loud-mouthed young man who had made the very most out of the damage his plane had suffered on the Duisburg trip. He'd put on his best uniform for this visit, the doctor noticed. To hear him talk in the Mess one would think he was fearless. Garrard watched the young pilot finger his tiny trimmed moustache. It seemed to Garrard that a man who trimmed his upper lip with such care and attention was possibly obsessive and certainly vain.

'Sleeping well?'

'As well as can be expected, sir.'

'What's that supposed to mean, then?'

'In view of the headaches.'

Garrard sniffed. Brent was what they called a Group A case. Flyers asking to be relieved of their duties – or who were suspected of wanting to be – were classified in four categories. Group A cases were men on their first few operations who had not been subjected to the serious stress of a bad crash, ditching or fire in the air, etc. Group As had the least excuse.

81

They heard a Lancaster open up to full revs, accelerate along the runway and then totter into the air. The noise made the windows rattle. 'Physically,' said Garrard, 'you're A1B, as far as I can find: fit for operational pilot duties.'

'Actually,' admitted Brent, 'I don't want to fly again.'

'Why not?'

'I've done three trips. I saw Gellespie go down over Krefeld, Doc. In flames; it wasn't pretty.'

'Everyone knows the feeling of fear, lad.'

'But each man does not fly,' said Brent.

'You chose to fly,' the doctor reasoned.

'I wanted to do my bit.'

'And you thought that flying would be . . .' the doctor hesitated before using the word, '. . . glamorous?'

'I didn't think it would be like this ghastly hole, like a fifth-rate factory on a commercial estate, cold and damp and bloody depressing.'

'And dangerous,' added Garrard.

'Not only dangerous. The planes go up into the dark rainy night and disappear as though the crews have never been born. Getting run over on the by-pass has more drama. A man's death should be more than that.'

'You're not a medical problem,' said Garrard.

'"For disposal by the executive",' quoted Brent.

The MO was surprised that Brent knew the very words that disclaimed medical responsibility and handed him over to disciplinary action and disgrace.

'You are suffering from a lack of confidence,' said Garrard. This too was the official terminology.

'You're bloody right I am, Doc. I've calculated that the average flying bod had a one-in-five chance of ending his tour in one piece.'

It was a bad sign when a flyer began to think in that way, but the doctor couldn't argue with the mathematics of it. Garrard said, 'My experience – which stretches over years of bomber operations – indicates that the anxieties you complain of are only temporary.'

Brent laughed ironically. 'Temporary! You're telling me; one in five against is only the *average*! A sprog like me can expect more like nine to one against.'

Garrard had meant nothing of that kind, but Brent's lucid fears began to affect the doctor. He said nothing. Brent spoke again. 'Suppose, Doc, that it was peacetime. A patient came to you and said he had a job on tall buildings. Suppose he said that four out of five workers were falling to their deaths because of faults in the girder construction. He tells you that he's feeling a bit anxious and that he'd feel a lot better in some other sort of employment. What would you tell him, Doc?' Brent smiled slightly and added, 'I mean, if you weren't an employee of the construction company.'

'You're a clever talker, Mr Brent,' said the doctor. He glanced down at the medical file and saw that Brent had been a salesman for electrical goods before the war. 'But you are not selling me a vacuum cleaner, you are trying to buy your skin at the expense of your comrades. We are not building a steel scaffolding, we are fighting a war for our lives. If we lose, God knows what will happen to all of us. Already we've seen what happened to Poland and France and the others that were beaten. Whatever the cost, our young men will give their lives because they believe they are fighting for God, or for their friends and their families.'

'All right, Doc. You believe that this faulty vision is my imagination. Well, perhaps you are right, but that doesn't make it any easier for me to judge my landings and take-offs. How would I feel at the controls of a bombed-up plane with my six-man crew all trusting in me when I know I'm not going to see properly?'

Garrard shuffled the papers on his desk. Brent had lost four pounds in weight since starting operations. It was a lot, but almost all the flyers lost a pound or two.

'You're refusing to fly?'

'Suppose there was a son of yours flying with me in my crew. What would your decision be then?'

'I'm not making a decision.'

'You are going to pass me over to the executive. They will crucify me.'

'There's no decision; I can't find anything wrong with you medically and I'll have to say so.'

'Just answer that question; suppose it was your kid in my rear turret?'

'My child is two years old, asleep in his cot at No 26 Officers' Married Quarters. It's just not possible for me to visualize the possibility. I'm sorry, Brent. Now, before I turn down your request to be medically grounded, why don't you forget the whole thing? I assure you that you're only going through a temporary worry. There's no need for anything to go on your documents. I'll mark you fit for flying and you'll go on the Battle Order without anyone knowing about our little chat.'

There was a long silence. Garrard said, 'You're looking for a deus ex machina.'

'I don't know what that is,' said Brent, his flat voice indicating that he had no curiosity about it.

'It's a device that writers use for making their plots end well.'

Brent grunted.

'An improbable device,' added Garrard, 'for bad writers and unlikely plots.'

Brent nodded. This upper-class gibberish was just Garrard's way of putting his knife in. Typically, it came complete with Latin tag and cigarettes that Garrard now held out to him in a slim gold case. Solid gold, not plated.

'Cigarette?' Brent took one and the doctor lit it for him. He noticed Brent's stained fingers and the covert way he held the cigarette after inhaling the smoke desperately. Sometimes a chap had to have a chance to say all the taboo things that were boiling up inside him. Garrard saw it as one of his more distasteful duties to face such scenes without flinching. Gellespie's session with him had been not unlike this, except that it all centred upon his newly born daughter. Relatives always added to the problems; for the flyers and Garrard and his staff. It wasn't fair.

They smoked in silence, and Garrard permitted himself to recall the early days of the war. The RAF had been a tiny exclusive club then: only a handful of bomber squadrons with smaller aircraft crewed by three or four men. At one time he'd known by sight almost every officer in the whole Command. Now the air force had been spoiled. There were thousand-bomber raids with seven men packed into each. Errand boys wore brevets for merely watching that engines didn't over-heat or tuning a wireless set. Briefings that had once been a crowd of carefree youngsters huddled around a table in the Operations Block before take-off had become 150 men sitting in the Station Cinema all the afternoon to be lectured in one-syllable words so that they would be sure to understand. If disliking that was snobbery, then Garrard would admit to being a snob, he'd often said so in the Mess.

This fellow Brent would never have lasted in one of the peacetime RAF squadrons. No Mess would have tolerated this windy, snivelling salesman. From his position behind the desk the doctor could see both himself and Brent reflected in the full-length mirror. No pair could be more different. Himself: plump and prematurely balding, already learning that stance that characterized the elderly medico, feet apart, one hand in the jacket pocket and the other flexing the stethoscope so that the ear plugs tapped together. Brent: the archetypal urban opportunist, undernourished and wiry, with a whining London accent that Garrard found unbearable. Brent was hunched forward in the chair as though he might suddenly burst into tears. It wouldn't be the first time that a flyer had done so, reflected Garrard, but if Brent did it the doctor would find it extremely distasteful. Brent would not weep the gracious tears that Rupert Brooke shed for England, it would be a shrill cry of self-pity.

For Brent the whole damned incoherent meeting went exactly as Sergeant Lewis – Brent's navigator – had warned it would. It was a well-known fact that Garrard was a peacetime airman who hated all civilians, especially those wearing air-force uniform. This stiff and unyielding doctor could never understand Brent's explanations. The only people who could get excused from operations without the terrible stain of LMF stamped on their documents were those who knew the secret language of the head-shrinkers. Fear was cowardice, but you might get away with anxiety; a pain in the guts was a visceral reaction, if you knew the lingo. It was all designed – Brent decided – to ensure that only public-school officers could get away with it.

Brent had never felt at ease as an officer. He should have stayed a flight sergeant, really. He was more at home in the Sergeants' Mess and he'd had more money in his pocket, too. These Officers' Mess charges were crippling on a flying officer's pay. On the other hand, no sergeant would stand the slightest chance of getting off ops on medical grounds. Sergeants were not considered sensitive enough to suffer a breakdown – what did they call it, trauma – or get migraine. These bloody witch-doctors with their fancy accents and their social pretensions made Brent see red. For a moment he was tempted to suggest that the doctor flew with them on the next trip. Doctors had flown on operations. Brent had heard of one who kept a graph of a crew's blood pressure and body temperature from take-off until return. Maybe this old bastard Garrard would like to observe Brent like that. How would he like a trip to Berlin and, perhaps, back? Just thinking of it made Brent sweat; he trembled and his eyelids fluttered and he felt the surge of nausea that he'd known on each trip. Even flying the air test produced the same effect. Whatever had persuaded him to volunteer for flying duties? Before the war he'd collected photos and cigarette cards of aeroplanes: Britain's Wonderful Air Force, fifty cards to a set. He had watched them write VAT 69 in white smoke over the rooftop of the miserable little house where he'd grown up. Aeroplanes then had seemed a way of escape from it all. Escape! More like a death sentence. The mere sound of the engines through the window made him acutely miserable.

Lancaster S Sugar taxied past. He heard the brakes squeal and the flip of throttle as it turned on to the straight part of the perimeter track that passed the Operations Block. He could see the blue sky and smell the freshly trimmed grass. Why for God's sake couldn't there be a break in this fine weather. In other summers he'd known July to be endless cloud and rain. Now that the aeroplane had passed he could hear the motor-mower pitter-pattering away over the airfield grass. He could have done his RAF service like that erk was doing his: driving a motor-mower into action and always returning unscathed for NAAFI break. And when the war was over, that erk would have an honourable discharge, all right. War service on an operational bomber station, conduct impeccable, moral fibre intact.

Jesus! I'll bet that fellow on the mower can tell a few stories when he's got a pint in his hand at the Bell. I'll bet he knows more about the strategy of heavy bombing than all the brass at High Wycombe. I'll . . . but suddenly Brent's hatred for the unknown airman was spent. He looked up to find the doctor staring at his hands. Self-consciously, Brent folded his arms, tucking the ugly fingers out of sight and clutching his chewed cuticles into the soft material of his sleeve. Grimy, scarred hands like Brent's were all right for mending the motor-cycle or fixing the wife's gas cooker, but they were out of place at the end of an officer's cuff. He looked at the doctor's soft black shiny shoes and contrasted them with his own cheap thick-soled 'war austerity' pattern. The doc was right, thought Brent, he had suffered a complete failure of confidence. He didn't feel able to pilot a four-engined bomber and command its crew. A captain needed more than skill; he needed the indefinable presence that good schools had provided for his fellow officers. Brent was inadequate, and every bloody aspect of the social system in which he'd grown up was anxious to rub it in.

Brent had been a door-to-door salesman of electric fires and gadgets before the war. And that wasn't something you could boast about over drinks in the anteroom. He felt ill at ease among these well-spoken men who had been solicitors, bank clerks, stockbrokers and civil servants. They were all grand jobs by Brent's definition, even if none of those men wanted to get back to their work as desperately as Brent wanted to get back to civvie street, and to Nelly and the kids. The phlegmatic way in which his middle-class comrades endured service life away from their be-gardened and multi-bathroomed homes and their loving prosperous families was a paradox that Brent was reconciled to never solving.

Revelation comes suddenly to men like Brent who are uninstructed in the intellectual progression of argument. Suddenly that afternoon he knew without any possible doubt that society wished to kill him. He had been designed like a bomb, long since costed and programmed on a graph of expendability. To object to flying was like asking that one of the 4,000-pound cookies now stored in the cool, dark, controlled air of the bomb store should be preserved for posterity. Why that one, they would ask, just as the doctor was now asking himself about Brent. Why this one, from among the thousands and thousands? The tax-payers have paid for his manufacture. He's the right weight, the right size, his powder is dry and his fuse is primed. Brent moved his leg into a beam of sunlight but felt no warmth.

The doctor studied the airman's face. His colouring was dark. No matter how carefully scoured, such a face would never look fresh and clean. The facial muscles were as tight as whipcord, and the bones were ridged with white as though about to burst through the skin.

Garrard looked down at the documents again. What sort of girl would have married him. 'Does your wife worry a lot?'

'Terrible. She's as thin as a rake. Doesn't get enough to eat, either. Gives her parents half her rations. I've told her over and over but she won't take no notice.'

Brent's wife lived close to the airfield, although it was against orders. She was more isolated by her husband's new rank than was Brent himself. She had tried, my God she had: whist drives, afternoon teas and even a committee. None of the other wives had been rude to her, but when she heard her own voice with its flat Midland vowels she became tongue-tied. Radio catch-words and jokey wartime slogans were no use to her when the others talked of books, and one interminable lesson convinced her that she would never learn bridge. Poor Nelly, but it wasn't fair that she should blame him.

'Have another try. It's never as bad as you think.'

Garrard remembered saying that very same thing to Gellespie. For one moment he felt guilty, but when Brent looked up and smiled, Garrard smiled too. The conversation was predictable. Men were depressingly alike, concluded the doctor.

'Suppose I kill someone?' said Brent.

'That's the whole idea.' Garrard moved forward and patted Brent's shoulder. It was a nervous gesture, as a timid child might touch a fierce dog. The young pilot put both hands up to his face. Garrard was afraid that he might sob, but a few seconds later his face emerged smiling and clear-eyed.

'Yes, that's the whole idea,' repeated the doctor. He decided to have a word with the CO and keep Brent off the Battle Order for a week. 'Take some exercise, get some fresh air into your lungs, try not to worry. I'll give you something to help you sleep.' The words came easily to him, for he had said them so many times to other frightened men.

'I'll give it a go,' said Brent.

Garrard nodded without hearing. Already his mind was occupied with other problems and other men.

Brent's Lancaster skewed across runway 27, took a corner off the Ops Block and demolished four houses in Officers' Married Quarters. It happened several times a week: sometimes Brent escaped unhurt, sometimes he was killed, but always the two-year-old son of the Medical Officer died in his pram. It happened in Brent's dreams, it happened every time he used that particular runway and it happened when he saw Dr Garrard in the Mess.

A man saves his most bitter hatred for those who have seen him at his most vulnerable, for those who despise him and for those who grant him a desperately needed favour. Brent had all those reasons for hating Garrard.

This hatred occupied all of Brent's mind and left no room for his fears of death.

He annoyed the Medical Officer by naming his bomber 'Deus ex machina' and having that written large across its nose. It was 'an improbable device for ending things', Brent explained in the Mess, and won an overnight reputation as a wag. He annoyed the Medical Officer by tucking his table napkin into his collar and telling dirty stories loudly in an exaggerated cockney accent. Brent knew that such behaviour was tolerated – and in fact applauded, by many of the young aircrew – as part of the tribute that operational crews exacted from Mess-mates who did not share their dangers. Brent also knew that he could behave like this only while he was acknowledged as one of the most valiant flyers on the squadron.

Thus Brent's DFC and later his DSO were by-products of his feud with Doctor Garrard. Brent admitted that he enjoyed announcing those awards in the hearing of the Medical Officer even more than he enjoyed telling his wife or his father.

A New Way To Say Goodnight

Two men in formal evening clothes crouched over the dying embers of a log fire and waited for half a dozen chestnuts to explode their nostalgic fragrance. The room was bare and cramped: a mere stone niche in a neo-Gothic façade. Upon the iron bedstead a thin blanket was turned back to reveal sheets that were grey and frayed. The cupboards were warped, the chairs rickety and under the cracked lino the floor was uneven. Yet such was the spell great universities cast upon even the proudest men, that the older man – the evening's guest of honour – felt a pang of envy for the life that this young Doctor of Philosophy led in a closed academic society.

Antique glass windows bent the Gothic cloisters and crippled the founder's statue that dominated the dark quadrangle. The gas lamps made yellow blotches in the mist, and footsteps clicked gently past as other scholars said goodnight to their guests. The young man was flattered that his eminent friend seemed to be in no hurry to depart. In the manner of a thoughtful host he poured more brandy into both glasses.

They had dined in the great hall, with paintings of the founder and this college's most famous sons looking down upon the timeless scene. The speeches had been urbane, and wittily sprinkled with classical pedantry of a sort that all present enjoyed. Yet the young man had become more and more aware that for his guest this was but a parochial corner in a vast and cosmopolitan world. He was envious and did nothing to conceal it as he stared at the older man. Still under forty, he was a Member of Parliament, and he'd won a chestful of medals before he was twenty-five, the boy's age. A good horseman and a crack shot, he devoted much of his time to wildlife preservation, and this evening had lectured those around him on the evils of vivisection. He was a skilled pilot, and knew enough about aviation to be a consultant to more than one manufacturer. He'd been an aviation journalist, too. He had a good memory for facts and figures and, like all good journalists, confidence enough to bridge the gaps so that the joins didn't show.

The boy looked closely at this middle-aged charmer with the low-set, rat-trap mouth that smiled so readily. And he listened to his stories. All through Europe he'd broken hearts by the dozen. He had met his wife after a forced landing on a frozen Swedish lake in a snowstorm: having secured his aircraft, he'd stayed that night at the near-by castle where the countess fell in love with him. The boy was pimply and bespectacled, with a nervous, girlish laugh; these stories reawakened the daydreams of his schooldays.

The two men could not have been more different. A life of study had made the boy thin and pale. The guest, despite his barrel chest, plump face and the fancy embroidery on his dress shirt, had the unmistakable bearing of a professional soldier. Yet he'd lived in Venice, spoke a gruff but efficient Italian and could talk on art treasures with authority, humour and enthusiasm. As a youth he'd been a mountaineer, and now, jealous voices said, he was a social climber of equal determination. Tonight he'd name-dropped shamelessly, exchanged dirty jokes and engaged in erudite argument with almost everyone in the Common Room, converting many of his political critics. The boy was proud of his guest and rediscovered within himself the heady symptoms of hero-worship. He fought them down.

'I suppose,' he said, 'it was different for your generation. There was so much of the world still unexplored,

93

so much that needed to be done.' A loud bang, as a chestnut exploded, made the soldier flinch. The boy used fire-tongs to get some chestnuts from the fire. The soldier took one in his bare hand, produced a pocket-knife and sliced it before tasting a piece.

He said, 'I'd been interested in flying for some time. The war enabled me to learn how, at government expense. I could never have afforded it otherwise. Flying is still a rich man's diversion, but it's fun – everyone should have a chance. After the war I remained in aviation and I used to see chaps I'd known in the squadron. I was interested in ex-servicemen, and sometimes I could help them find jobs or advise them about pensions. It was those ex-servicemen who influenced me to go into politics proper, I suppose. Or, rather, their problems. I was surprised to get elected so easily; after all, I'm not a polished speaker, and I'm no good at all at kissing babies . . . except female ones born about eighteen years ago.' He got up from his seat at the fire, smoothed his suit and ran his stubby white fingers along the books on the mantelpiece. There was all the predictable stuff: textbooks, Karl Marx, girly magazines and detective stories. The soldier selected an Agatha Christie. 'I've read that; I guessed who did it. I'm re-reading all my Dashiell Hammett at the moment.' He turned back to the boy suddenly enough to make him jump. 'What about politics, then?'

'I've read Lenin and Marx and *Mein Kampf*, and I belong to the Liberal Club here in college,' said the boy defensively.

The soldier smiled sardonically. 'Marx seems pretty fashionable here at the moment.'

'The left-wing people dress rather wildly, so you notice them more. Last week they staged a demonstration in my lecture. They brought in red flags and sang the *Internationale*.'

There was a long silence. The boy felt uneasy with this powerful figure behind him. He remembered his childhood fears of being strangled in his sleep. In those nightmares also his assailant had been a giant with soft white hands. The relationship between the two men was tacitly agreed. The soldier had chosen his man well.

'What did you do?' The soldier's voice was soft and friendly.

'There's not much one *can* do. We are instructed not to provoke the students, ever since those three were injured last term. I packed up my books and notes and left them to it.'

'Many of your class were active in the demonstration?'

'About a third.'

'And so the majority lose a lecture because of them? It's a bad business, Chris.' It was the first time the soldier had addressed him informally. Chris wondered whether he was expected to reciprocate, but decided against doing so before being invited. Soldiers were rather old fashioned in some things, in spite of this one's friendly informality.

'It's not just in the colleges, though,' said the boy.

The soldier rubbed his face as though he was suddenly very tired. 'No, Chris, it isn't. The whole damned world has gone mad, I'm afraid.'

'What will happen?'

'God alone knows, Chris. The trouble is, one can see the point of view of all of them. We have long since entered a technical age; the world is linked by fast transport and the craftsman is on the way to extinction, perhaps for ever. During the industrial revolution capitalists exploited workers until they drew blood. Now it seems to be labour that has the upper hand. The trade unions are exacting a terrible revenge upon our whole economy. But there is a point beyond which capital won't go. The sort of new ideas and new industries we need must have high-risk capital investment. World competition is fiercer than it has ever been before. Nowadays the investor has too many ways of losing his money and not enough to make more.'

'Perhaps the state should be the investor.'

'It's a fine theory, but it doesn't work. Look at state-run industries, not just here at home but overseas, too. There's not one of them that can hold a candle to the better private companies. No state employee will take a risk or back a hunch like the individual investor. Call it greed or avarice, but the fact is that the state employee has nothing to gain and everthing to lose by backing an unusual idea.'

'Some of the students think that only a return to religion will solve things.'

'And I agree, Chris, but it will have to be a religion that is in tune with the age in which we live. It must make people show their love for their neighbour by co-operation with their neighbour. Our people must rejoice in the simple things of life: their families, the countryside, craftsmanship and the satisfaction of hard work.'

'It sounds a bit grim, sir.'

'I hope it doesn't, Chris. This is the way to greatness. You can't tell me that youngsters enjoy this permissive society we're hearing about all the time. If the kids were jumping in and out of bed in a multiple orgy of endless happiness then perhaps I'd modify my views, but they all seem so bloody unhappy. In the High Street of this little university town there are at least three shops selling pornographic books and photos. Even in the newsagent there are sex books mixed up with the children's comics and nudie magazines alongside the newspapers. And yet the atmosphere among these students is of impending doom.'

'Students do have problems, sir.' The boy removed his gold-rimmed spectacles and polished them with a yellow silk handkerchief that he kept solely for that purpose.

'So I keep hearing, Chris. Students think that they are the only people fit to rule the world, and to prove it they spend their days in drugged idleness.'

'And you have the solution, sir?'

'You're angry with me now. I can hear it in your voice. You think I'm an old fogey trying to sell you hard work and obedience.'

Chris shook his head to deny this. His guest picked up a hot chestnut and peeled it without hesitation. In the firelight he looked particularly handsome, his long wavy hair showing not a trace of grey. For a moment he looked pained as he relived a memory. 'My God, Chris, I could tell the world a few things about hard drugs. When I was badly wounded they shot me full of morphine. The pain was so bad that I needed it for months. I became an addict. But I cured myself. It's simply a matter of will-power. That's all it is.' He picked up the poker to prod the dying fire. As he waved it to emphasize his point the boy recoiled. When the boy spoke his voice betrayed his nervousness. 'Drugs are not the biggest problem facing us.'

'I agree. The most immediate danger is subversion. There is a Red Menace, and don't let anyone persuade you differently. The Russians are not fools. Quite apart from the noisy idiots who think they are communists, and the film stars who like to get their photos in the papers, and the noisy hooligans who just want to get into a punch-up with the police, there are the silent plotters who are truly hoping to take over the government. These people are the dangerous ones and they must be neutralized.'

'Even at the expense of parliamentary democracy?'

'Especially at the expense of parliamentary democracy. These people have spent their lives acquiring protective colouring that makes them almost invisible in a parliamentary democracy.'

97

'You'd make political activity illegal?'

'We'd make political activity *unnecessary*. We must get the country running again. In the beginning it would simply mean paying a fair wage for a fair day's work and leaving the idle to starve. The idle in this case would be anyone who does not contribute directly to the prosperity of the country, whether he's a financier or a shop steward.'

'But what about wives and dependants? What about the sick and what about the poor?'

The soldier had nursed the wife he'd loved through years of grave sickness. Recently she had died and still he'd not grown used to the silence of his house. 'Whatever have people told you about me?' He smiled sadly. 'At least a dozen times I've pawned this watch to pay the grocer. Look closely and you'll see the pawn-broker's secret scratches on the gold case.' For a moment he looked at his watch as if seeing those scratches for the first time. When he spoke again it was without raising his eyes from it. 'I believe our people are fine people: the finest people in the whole world. The old and the sick and the lame must be cared for, cared for better than ever before. But in order to do this the fit must work.'

'What if they can't get a job?'

'The state must provide jobs. With one or two exceptions our roads are still fit only for horse and cart. The whole country should have good roads and larger airports, and there will always be work to do on them. Then there is the land. Agriculture must be revitalized. Nowadays many of the jobs are done by machines, but only the finest of our soil is being used. We must exploit our resources to the full. We don't have silver or gold but we do have a kind climate so we must use as much of our land as possible. In all these matters we must call in the experts, and instead of filing their reports away, we must act on them.'

'I certainly agree with that. It's tragic the way government after government ignores the warnings that the experts give them.'

The young man poured another drink for them both. The soldier sipped briefly before going on. 'Nothing that we plan to do is anything but common sense. You'd be surprised how many socialists – when speaking privately – agree that the power of the trade unions must be reduced if we are to export our goods at prices that can compete with the rest of Europe. Quite a few liberals are prepared to acknowledge that crime and disorderly conduct among young people and students can only be remedied by giving the police force a chance to do its job without endlessly sniping at them. This is a new age we are entering, Chris. No one can be more aware of the energy, ideals and enthusiasm of young people than you fellows at our universities. But after youngsters have spent three long years learning ethics, truth and justice we turn them out into the cold grey world of avarice and opportunism. Is it any wonder that they become cynical? Is it surprising that there are so many young criminals today? Violent criminals? We want to use that energy and idealism. We want to make our youth into constructive citizens, who will be proud to work hard and share in the prosperity that results. This is the new sort of socialism that our party are working for.'

'It sounds good,' admitted Chris.

'Sounds good!' beamed the older man. 'You sound like the cynical war veteran that the newspapers say I am!'

'It's true, what you say. Everyone agrees that this country is down to its last chance.'

The soldier reached towards the boy and then stopped. He pointed his finger. 'Then let's *take* the chance, Chris. We are on the eve of a revolution.'

'What am I supposed to do about it? The university frowns on political activity by the faculty.'

'And so it should, Chris. I'm not suggesting that you get yourself mixed up with electioneering, distributing handbills or listening to endless speeches in draughty village halls. But we want serious young people to join our movement – '

'Your religion, you mean.'

The soldier laughed. 'Religion, I should have said. We want young people of all kinds and classes. If there's one thing that's holding this country back, it's the class system, and that's something we are determined to end. We want farm hands and clerks, garage mechanics and graduates, no matter what were their previous politics. We are concerned only about tomorrow. The chaps we already have working with us are as varied as can be: business-men, miners, builders and professors are on our commit-tees. What you can do, Chris, is to ask the best of the best of your students to come along and hear for them-selves what we have to say.'

'You want me to select them?' Chris asked.

'We don't want Marxists, who come only to break up our meetings, if that's what you mean. Send me warriors.'

'No Jews or Catholics?'

'We want converts,' said the soldier, 'not evangelists for other faiths.' He stood up and reached for his over-coat. 'It's been a fine evening. I don't remember when I last heard such stimulating conversation at dinner.'

'I'll do as you ask. At this stage in our history we must all be bold.'

'That's true,' said the soldier putting on his fur-lined trench coat and soft hat. 'Two many men have equivo-cated too many times. Now we must act.'

'I'll apply for membership,' said the young man. 'It can be kept confidential, I suppose?' Through the door he could see his guest's new black Mercedes.

'It can and will, Chris.'

'Goodnight, Captain Göring. Thank you for coming.'

'It was my pleasure,' said the man. 'But if you are joining us, you must start using our form of greeting.'

'Heil Hitler,' said the young man.

'Heil Hitler,' said the Captain Göring.

Lord Nick Flies Again

A smile played around the courtly features of Lord Nick as he pulled his deerstalker hat down upon his be-goggled face.

'That's my idea of a binge, gentlemen,' he called, as he disappeared into the clouds above the Strait of Dover. You could say what you liked about Captain Lord Nicholas Beau-de-Ville, fourteenth Earl of Inverness, who had left Her Majesty's Foot Guards under a cloud after winning the VC in Africa, but by golly he could certainly make his flying-machine cavort through the clouds like an eagle. His years spent building the torpedo-shaped craft in a secret cave on his Highland estates had paid dividends. Using a secret gas to render the population unconscious but unharmed, he had swooped upon the Paris Mint, the German Emperor's castle and even the Home Fleet drawn up in review order in the Solent. Within a few weeks he had amassed plunder beyond compare, and each time he made his escape into the puffy white clouds that the artist invariably used to conceal the more technical aspects of the great mechanical bird. For Lord Nick, nattily clad in well-cut Norfolk jacket and riding-boots, had flown through the pages of *British Boy's Comic* long before the Wright brothers had built their less versatile machine.

When, at his prep school, Peter Wright read 'The Exploits of Lord Nick – Aviator' he'd never dreamed that before he was old enough to vote he would be in control of a flying-machine and heading across that same sea himself. And, to use Lord Nick's favourite endorsement, it was a binge; a ripping binge.

From the seat of his Sopwith Camel, Peter Wright could reach almost as far as the lower wing. It vibrated with a steady drumming noise as the air stream hammered on the fabric, stretched tight by the shiny dope. Near Boulogne an acre of glasshouses reflected the sun. The light came right through the wing and drew a crisp pattern of wooden spars, struts and ribs upon the golden fabric. He didn't need reminding that he was carried through the sky by a bundle of spruce sticks and a few yards of cloth. The sunlight even showed the carefully darned patches where it had been shot up and torn and neatly stitched by deft-fingered riggers. Such a tiny machine would fit easily into his mother's kitchen at Farm Lane. It dipped and yawed as it encountered the uncertain support of a fast-moving thermal. The bracing wire slackened as the lower wing met the rising air, then all were as taut as a cat's cradle again. Peter corrected the joystick until the wing-tips rested close upon the horizon. If it were his bus he'd have her rigged tighter than this; far tighter. He moved the rudder to turn the coastline under him and be rid of the glare that edged his aeroplane with haloes of sunlight. Carefully, he centred the stick. On a left-hand turn, the torque of a rotary engine could whip a Camel into a fatal spin unless a pilot handled it with respect. 'As touchy as a whore in a battleship,' his instructor had told him. Peter would have expected a whore in a battleship to be rather mellow, but as a pupil pilot of eighteen years, in a Mess full of veterans, he had kept his thoughts to himself.

Air flowed over the aeroplane like water; it rippled, gushed and tumbled over struts, stays and the edges of his windscreen with a noise like a waterfall. It sang in the wires. Childishly, Peter bent his head to enjoy the force of the airflow, letting it scream over his ear-flap and pummel his cheeks so that the goggles bit into his face.

He'd never flown over the sea before; very few men had. Everywhere the colours were most intense and yet more delicate than any he'd seen from under the dusty air that earthbound men thought was sky. The horizon was banded cobalt, azure, pearl and then a trace of pink before it changed to the tropical blue of the distant ocean. Yet fifteen thousand feet directly below him the sea was not blue; it was grey and lifeless. He squinted into the pink band to find the coast of Kent. On his map he'd pencilled a course that brought a landfall just west of Folkestone. Ashford should appear after that. Then he'd only to follow fifty miles of straight railway track due west of Farnborough aerodrome. He'd committed the flight plan to memory so that he wouldn't need to refer to his map. Last month, east of Arras, the air stream had whipped a map out of his hands. The flight commander had made a terrible fuss about it. If it had happened over the enemy lines, just a few miles away, it would have meant a court martial.

Still the endless sea; a pattern of spume showed the force and direction of the wind. The engines hiccupped and the boy blipped the throttle wide open. There was a sudden smell of the ether-and-alcohol mixture. The motor coughed again before it picked up and roared at the higher revs. Perhaps it was just a bit of dirt. The extra speed had put his nose up and he pressed the stick forward a fraction. Perhaps it was moisture from the patch of cloud he'd flown through on the other side of St Omer. Cloud did that sometimes.

Far to his right he could still see the French coast like a dribble of grey ink brushed upon wet paper. At this height – fifteen thousand feet – he found it difficult to breathe. One of the chaps had said that they should have parachutes when they took these old biplanes back to England, but he'd been shouted down by the other pilots. Parachutes were all right for balloonists but infra dig for pilots. Anyway, a parachute wouldn't be much use here, fifteen thousand feet above the sea. Eighteen thousand feet he should have said; he'd climbed since the last time he'd looked at his altimeter. He tapped the glass and the needle dropped a few hundred feet. It was a crude instrument, but he could feel from the softness of the controls that he was very high. He pulled his scarf down and gulped air into his oxygen-starved lungs. Camels weren't good above fifteen, that's why the Huns were so keen to entice them high. That's what had happened in August when his chums, Nigel and Charles, had been shot down.

The motor was spluttering a little. That too was probably the altitude, and yet he didn't fancy going any lower. If something did happen he wanted to be able to glide as far as possible. He glanced back to the French coast again. The last smudge of it was floating back under his tail. From under the trailing edge of the port wing crept a grey feathery wake which narrowed and became whiter until the grey-steel arrowhead of a troopship was its tip. The Boulogne–Folkestone blighty boat; he'd crossed four times on it. There was a destroyer escort, too. At 100 mph he soon left them behind on the cold, grey, empty sea. He leaned to one side to see round the guns. In spite of the red silk scarf that he'd wrapped around his face, he met the acrid smell of scorching oil. She was overheating. He reached forward to touch the metal cowling. He could feel it warm through the thick leather gauntlet gloves.

Nervously, he reached for the spark control and advanced it but he couldn't be sure that the motor was running better. Its tremendous noise stunned the eardrums and made it as hard to hear as endless glare made it difficult to see. He wished he'd never volunteered to bring this Camel to England but it was such a coincidence:

105

Wright. Farm Lane, Potten near Farnborough, Hants
MAKE A BIRTHDAY CAKE BUT DON'T SEND IT.
LOVE AND KISSES

PETER

His mother might not immediately guess that his telegram meant that he would be home on his nineteenth birthday, but his father would. The trouble was that these old crates sent back to Farnborough for complete overhaul were usually in rough condition. The fitter and riggers would not spend the usual care and attention on a scout that they would never service again.

Crikey, she was getting hot now; spluttering like a consumptive tram car. Less throttle. Major Mason would have taken this one, if there hadn't been another to go back next week that would give him three days in London instead of a measly four hours in Farnborough. Anyway, this would do for Peter. His family hadn't seen him since he'd got his second pip. If only he had a medal to show them, too; but that would come. He twisted his body anxiously to scan the entire horizon. Then he smiled at his own nervousness. Zeppelins and Gothas had crossed the North Sea on bombing raids, but they'd not venture as far south as this.

Bang. Bang-bang. The motor backfired and rocked the whole airframe, but before he could do anything about it the rhythm returned to its normal beat. There was enough smoke to make him anxious, and by now he was convinced that the spark adjustment made no difference. The engine was filthy with hardened oil deposit which prevented the valves seating properly. That caused the backfires and the constant smell of unburned fuel. He pushed the oil-spattered goggles up to his forehead and half closed his eyes, trying to see the English coast.

In mid-Channel he'd prayed only to get as far as the coast, but when he saw Folkestone creep under his starboard wing his troubles were not over. He followed the coast past Hythe but could not see the airfield at Lympne. He should have taken special note of the airfields en route, but it was too late to do anything about that now. The Camel wasn't the sort of bus that would forgive a pilot who tried to get a map from his bag while flying one-handed.

He put her nose down into the coastal haze and flew along the beach. He saw castellated mansions and a vast red hotel with flags flying. Not far from Dymchurch bathing-machines were lined up on the strand while the attendants rode the horses across the shingle and into the sea. No chance of putting his little machine down upon that strip of seashore. He banked steeply and turned away across the marshes, flying low enough to put the birds up and bring the people out of their cottages. He found a railway line and followed it as far as Ashford station. There was a train at the platform, its smoke rising vertically. Circling until he could be certain of the sign ASHFORD on the platform, he brought her nose until it pointed west. Under him the railway stretched as straight as could be, as far as the horizon.

Isolated from the people on the ground, both physically and by what he had seen of the filth and agonies of war, he viewed them now with the detachment that he would have accorded tropical fish in an aquarium. There were punts on a small back-water. Dressed in muslin, girls reclined, and men in coloured blazers laughed in a way that he'd forgotten. A goggled man in a powerful motor – longer than his Camel – thought he was trying to race him. He took up the challenge along the London road, but Peter's route carried him away until car and dust were lost behind the trees. A solitary cyclist made him remember his days at college. It was as if he'd been given a chance to look at himself and his innocent pre-war world. Some of the men had returned from leave angry that life in England made only perfunctory acknowledgment of the war. But Peter didn't want anything here to change. He wanted it preserved unaltered.

There was a crowd on Farnborough aerodrome by the time he reached it. They'd even come out of the Mess. His anxiety had sharpened his reactions and he came on to finals with a minimum of fuss. The engines sounded rougher as he throttled back and let her drift down. There was no wind at all, and at the last minute he had to open up for fear of brushing the hedge near the main road. Always tail-heavy, the Camel didn't like that sort of treatment and she reared. He cut the motor and she stalled, dropping like a stone. There was a spine-jarring bump and the port wing-tip almost touched the ground. They couldn't have seen that from the other side of the field, for the wheels, passing over an old cart track, had kicked up enough dust to hide him. After the scout settled, he gunned her back across the oily grass that flattened in the slipstream. While losing speed he kicked on right rudder to counteract the engine torque. Little blips of throttle made the stick twitch in his hands. He flicked the brass mag switches off. The prop jerked to a stop. Peter pulled the clip of the Sutton harness. Suddenly it seemed very quiet, excect for the singing of the birds.

'You're the officer taking the SE back to St Omer?' The Sergeant fitter saluted as Peter gripped the polished wooden centre-section struts and climbed out of the cockpit. The wickerwork seat creaked loudly. Two mechanics held the wing-tips and another fellow pushed the chocks tight under the wheels. Peter took the large watch out of its clip on the instrument panel. There was more fuss if one of those was lost than if a whole aeroplane was written off.

'Is it ready?' He pulled his flying-helmet off to hear better and undid his heavy leather flying-coat.

'Nearly ready,' said the sergeant as he steadied his

arm. He looked at Wright's RFC jacket. A novice; the real old timers wore their old regimental jackets with wings. Peter's new high-buttoned double-breasted design marked him as a latecomer to the war.

'A couple of hours?' said Peter.

'Give us three, sir.'

'If I can't leave by four o'clock I'll go tomorrow.' Only fools, birds and Zeppelins were flying after dark.

'Perhaps we'd better say tomorrow, sir?' said the Sergeant. Peter looked at him. He was a grey-haired man with pre-war campaign ribbons on his tunic. His wrinkled hands were deeply ingrained with oil stains except where corns and scars made smooth, white patterns. He smiled. At home he had a schoolboy son who looked as old as this pink-faced lieutenant.

'I'm going to see my parents.'

'How far is that, sir.'

'Five miles.' Peter stuffed his flying-helmet and scarf into his flying-coat pocket and took his forage cap from his tunic shoulder strap in such a way that the Sergeant could glimpse his second pip. To impress his parent's he'd put on his Sam Browne belt and his new boots and breeches.

'There's an Enfield motor-bike outside the hangar. The Orderly Officer uses it for his rounds. If you phone the Officers' Mess he'll probably lend it to you.'

'I say! I'll do that.' Everthing was working out wonderfully well.

The smelly little biplane was making bell-like noises as its motor cooled. Nose and wing were spattered with the castor oil that the Clerget drank so greedily. He could smell it on his overcoat, too.

'Good trip?' The Sergeant pointed to the Camel. The riggers were pushing it towards the hangar. One man supported the tail with only one hand. To Peter it seemed a miracle that this frail contraption had taken him all the way from northern France to his home here in England. He wanted to explain his feelings to this Sergeant. He wanted to say something appropriate to the miracle of a flight across an ocean. He searched his memory for a quotation that might convey the depth and intensity of his emotions. The Sergeant waited for an answer.

'It was a binge,' said Lieutenant Wright.

Discipline

There was no discipline. On paper they were an Illinois regiment of infantry, but a glance would have told any soldier that they were a rag-tag outfit with nothing that might hold them together when they made contact with the enemy. You could see it in the way they came up the hill that morning. They moved like a rabble, ignoring commands and straggling over three miles. A homestead was fired on the left flank and there was some brawling in the yard. Fifty of the soldiers had come out of that mêlée with chickens. There is no word that tells what those fifty men had in commmon. They were certainly not the most hungry men, nor were they the strongest. They were not exactly the most ruthless nor entirely the most self-interested, but whatever quality they shared they recognized it among themselves and wore their spoils at their belts proudly, as Indian braves wore scalps.

Of Sergeant Winkelstein's company, four soldiers had chickens. These four stood close together and watched their Sergeant as he came across the field towards them. The tallest of the four was Private Green. He was the only man in the regiment with two chickens.

'They say the Sergeant was in a shooting war in Europe afore he came out here,' said Private Joshua Ashton.

'Winkelstein?' said Private Green. He repeated the name several times as if struggling to find the correct way to pronounce it. 'Like hell he was.' Green spat. They were all proud of their Anglo-Saxon names; they grinned.

'Goddamned *Jäger*,' said Bray. He used the word with a mixture of awe and contempt, as his parents had used it. Jägers were the German mercenary soldiers whom the British had brought here to suppress the American colonists. They had failed.

'Winkelstein's from Philadelphia,' said Ashton.

'With that accent? The teamsters on the chow wagon are all from Philly. You ever hear them talk like Sergeant Winkelstein?' Green spat again. There had been a time, only a week before, when the others would have stepped back to avoid staining their uniform, but now they no longer cared.

'Sure acts like he was in a shooting war; runs around squealing like a pregnant sow.' Ashton slapped at the horse-flies around his face. There were so many of them that it made no difference.

'Here comes the midget himself,' said Green.

Karl-Heinz Winkelstein was a short thickset man of thirty-two. A pork butcher by training and a civilian by instinct, this was the third time he'd served in the Union Army.

He'd served his first term with the 69th New York Regiment. Its enlisted time had expired before the first battle of Bull Run. Curiosity rather than valour had prompted most of the regiment to extend their service in order to take part in the battle. Both armies were ardent novices, stumbling about in confusion and dying by the hundreds because they didn't know enough about war to know it was time to run away. It was early afternoon when Winkelstein decided not to further extend his contract with the Union. The 8th New York Regiment were firing at him in error. Some of the Union Army wore a shade like Confederate Grey, and some of the reb regiments wore blue. Soon the men around him were firing at anyone they saw. Then a group of the youngest soldiers threw away their guns and ran.

To the east of the battlefield the slanting meadows were a patchwork quilt of luncheon parties from Washington. The picnickers' Sabbath was disturbed by a routed army that ploughed right through them. The men of Winkelstein's company did not rest until they reached the bank of the Potomac.

Winkelstein worked as a waiter in one of Washington's best restaurants, but after losing six months' savings in a faro club he decided to rejoin the Army of the Potomac for the sake of the three-hundred-and-fifty-dollars bounty. For six more months he jealously clung to his job as an army supply clerk and thus stayed in the city, but in August his luck ran out. He arrived at McClellan's headquarters with a wagon train of bacon and grain just in time to get a Springfield and bayonet, a bandolier of bullets and two days' rations and he hurried to the battle of Antietam. His slight limp was a remembrance of that day when he vowed he'd never wear uniform again. After four weeks in a Philadelphia hospital he'd walked out without permission and got back to New York and his uncle on 14th Street. He'd worked as a butcher and lived with the family for almost a year.

Then the Federal Government pased the conscription laws. In spite of the great riots – when the city of New York passed into the hands of the draft protestors for several days – Winkelstein, and most of the rest of them, had been drafted into the army. No one had asked him about previous military experience, but his ability to read and write gave him sergeant's rank in a regiment of illiterate conscripts. It was an unenviable job.

Winkelstein's face was small and round: porcine, almost, like the pigs that had hung eviscerated in his uncle's shop. His hair was greying and his face untanned. In the city it had been a status symbol to remain unmarked by the sun under which manual labourers toiled, but here it was just one more physical characteristic that marked him as different to the men he commanded. Worse still, his skin was going bright red and blistering, so that he appeared constantly to be in an apoplectic rage.

And yet he tried to be a better Sergeant than the ones he had served under. This unit consisted mostly of farm boys. The rest were village kids: grocers, barbers, even a banjo-player. *Ach weh*! They would never be any good as soldiers: not them, not him, not anyone here, not even Lieutenant Simms, his officer.

The four soldiers began to dig as the Sergeant approached, but after he'd passed they straightened up, wiped the sweat from their faces and squeezed their hands against their aching back muscles. Already that morning they had dug four such holes. They had dug holes down near the creek and behind the railroad junction where they had arrived. Then they had marched up here to dig holes again. The men conserved their energies and did little more than scratch the topsoil.

The valley was five miles long and one mile wide, most of it visible from their lines on the crest of the eastern hills. These hills were a small wrinkle of the vast Appalachian range of mountains: a Mesozoic pucker made when the earth was young and tender. Their coniferous skyline made the distant hills into soft blue saws, bent in the knee of the land and ready to sing. The nearest of the hilltops – just a mile as the crow flies from where the soldiers waited – was green and treeless. This was the place the men's eyes constantly returned to. It was here that the enemy would appear.

A hot summer had turned the slopes of this valley a thousand shades of yellow. Grass had scorched to hay, the rocks were ugly sulphurous outcrops that almost matched the canary-coloured flowers of the gorse bushes. Even on the lower slopes, where the muddy waters might have made the vegetation green, ochreous dust continued the unremitting scheme of yellows.

The dirty river meandered through the valley, half hidden by trees and bushes like a cobra in the grass. Its tail was narrow, and spumed white between the rocks,

114

but its hood spread wide and disappeared into groves of hemlock trees. Joshua Ashton had a good eye for swampland. His brother had died in such a place back home in Michigan. The Frenchies called them *savanes*, and sometimes the danger-signals were groves of cedars or tamaracks. Ashton had earned his living from timber, as had his entire family, all thirteen of them. Here, though, there were trees he did not recognize. There were so many more varieties than back home, from the hard dark-green shapes of the conifers all the way to the feathery beeches, their leaves holding the sunshine captive and gleaming like newly minted coins. These trees grew in mixed clumps. A man would have a hard time living from such woodland.

Joshua Ashton looked at the tree nearest to him. It had a graceful curve in its upper third. Back home he would have earmarked such a tree. In a couple of years' time it could make a set of shafts for a fine wagon. Here there were no fine wagons, just the clumsy army design, made in a factory six at a time by townsmen who would never be craftsmen like the Ashtons.

'You got any of those reb cigars left, Josh?' asked Green.

'No,' said Ashton automatically, as they had all learned to do since joining the army. Green knew he had some left and continued as if the answer had been in the affirmative.

'I'll bet you four of them to four pair of wollen socks that the German midget ain't with us no more come Thursday dinner.'

Ashton calculated how much time that would give Green to wreak his promised magic. 'What are you going to do?' he asked.

'That'd be telling, Josh. Bet?'

'Three cigars . . . and no holes in the socks, mind.'

115

'Done,' said Green. He called across to Bray. 'You hear that, Bray?'

'I heard you,' said Bray. 'Thursday dinner.'

'Him or me,' said Green with a swagger. 'That's the way I figured with the drillmaster: him or me.'

Everyone remembered the bullying drillmaster at recruit camp. Green had only spoken with him in private for five minutes, but the man had asked for compassionate leave and left the camp not to return until after Green and the rest of them had completed their two weeks' training.

At 9.30 A.M. the train arrived. They saw it coming when it was still miles away. It was a strange-looking beast, its cow-catcher grinning and the huge funnel-shaped smoke-stack belching fumes and sparks like a volcano. It came close enough for the soldiers to see passengers standing on the observation platforms at the end of each coach. The women were in coloured silk dresses and the men in shiny stovepipe hats and frock-coats. Some of the women waved to the soldiers. No one waved back; they could not completely believe in what they saw.

The rain stopped at the water-tank. Without the cooling speed of the wind, the carriages became hot and airless under the hard white sun. The blinds of the windows were pulled down and no one alighted from the train except one elderly carpetbagger who stretched his legs briefly before climbing back inside. When the water was aboard, the locomotive gave a whoop and a roar like a war-party. Then there was a burst of steam that made the wheels spin. It did the same again and then slowly pulled away, its bell ringing a joyful carillon. Joshua Ashton returned to his digging, but the edge of his spade was bent and he made slow progress into the hard stony earth.

'Cavalry are moving off,' said Green. He was a lazy

man in spite of his huge muscles and towering height. His face was wrinkled from the sunlight and scarred from fist fights, and his teeth were stained brown from chewing tobacco. At twenty-eight his skin was already marked by the purple tinge and broken veins of the heavy drinker. So was his father's face, and his uncle's, too, and yet both men were over eighty and still working. And still fathering children.

Green's eyes were beautiful: pale and clear, like a stream of mountain water. They were also insolent and chilling. Many people – including Sergeant Winkelstein – had described them as killer's eyes. Green knew this, and he used his arrogant unwinking stare as a weapon to intimidate any man who measured less than six feet three inches.

He leaned on his pickaxe and watched the troop of cavalry picking its way carefully up the slope behind them. Green could handle a horse better than any of the men he'd yet seen among the cavalry, or at least so he claimed; there was not a man among his company who'd not heard him say so a dozen times. To show his contempt for the horsemanship of the troop, Green spat tobacco juice into the hole he'd started to dig. Then he picked up his faded uniform jacket and put it on. No one had to tell him that the fighting would start soon. It was in the air, along with the birdsong, grass seeds and the flies that bit deep enough to draw blood. The other soldiers had also been digging stripped to their undervests, and now they followed Green's example and began to put on their heavy serge coats. None of them fitted their owners well for none of the jackets were new. Several bore crusty brown stains in the linings. Green's jacket hardly covered his behind and with the belt tight around his waist it stuck out like a ballerina's skirt, but no one had ever displayed any amusement at Green's incongruous appearance.

Sergeant Winkelstein marched back along the line of infantry, checking the depth of the holes. Few were deeper than two feet. Winkelstein tutted. He knew that Lieutenant Simms would be angry.

Winkelstein had bought a pair of German field glasses from a soldier at the Assembly Camp. Now he used them to study the bald hilltop that faced them. Only an army of fools would attempt to approach the floor of the valley to retake the railroad, and Johnny Reb was no fool. Especially when he was fighting in terrain he knew so well.

Winkelstein turned back to his men. The four soldiers near the dead horse were his worst problem. One of them – Green – was a giant with fists like pork hocks. Winkelstein knew that he could cripple any man in the company with one blow. Joshua Ashton – the Michigan boy – would have made a good soldier but for Green. The other two, Harvey and Bray, were silly country kids who saw Green's insolence as both entertaining and admirable.

Winkelstein shouted, 'The trench must be five feet deep!' Some of the soldiers grinned. Winkelstein flushed. He knew his accent sounded strange to these young boys who had never been far from home and family until now. Some of the others had seen music-hall comedians with routines that involved funny German patter. He'd seen them himself in New York.

'You must dig,' shouted Winkelstein.

The men muttered as they took off their jackets again. Green said something, and the other three roared with laughter and then looked up at Sergeant Winkelstein to see how he would react.

'Green,' shouted Winkelstein.

'Yes, Sergeant Winkelstein?' drawled Green. Somewhere someone laughed, but Winkelstein knew he must not turn his head away from Green. The buzzing of the insects was loud underfoot. The soldiers made no sound.

'What did you say, Green?'

'I said, "Some of the soldiers won't be able to see out, if we dig her five feet deep," said Green. He grinned. Winkelstein was the only man in the company who was shorter than five feet nine inches. Winkelstein was five feet four.

'You want to give me trouble, Green?' said Winkelstein.

Green shrugged. Along the road behind them there came four Whitworth twelve-pounder guns. The horses were frothing at the bit and the cannons were so heavy that the ground shook underfoot. For a moment there was too much noise to hear a man speak. As the guns passed, a cloud of light-brown dust enveloped Winkelstein and his men before rolling gently down the slope and being swallowed by the light breeze that was coming from the south-east.

'Start digging,' shouted Winkelstein again. He said it to the whole line of men and turned away from Green in pretended concern with Lieutenant Simms whom he saw riding up the cart track behind them. The other soldiers followed his gaze and when they saw the officer they began to put on a show of working hard so that any complaints by Winkelstein would seem underserved.

'I've just come from the Colonel,' said Lieutenant Simms.

Winkelstein snapped his fingers. It was a waiter's gesture. Joshua Ashton smiled as he took the reins of the Lieutenant's little Indian skewbald pony and steadied her while the officer dismounted. Lieutenant Simms's uniform was a magnificent affair. He'd been with a volunteer regiment from New York when the war started and they had designed their own. The dark-blue frock-coat, light-blue trousers and white gauntlets were the same as the rest of the Federal Army, but his sleeves were faced with gold Austrian knots and he wore a white sash round his waist under the leather belt that supported a sabre.

Sergeant Winkelstein remembered the colours of his officer's uniform, but a stranger would not have known. The white gauntlets were stained brown from the dubbin on his reins and their fingers were gashed and torn. His trousers had faded to a light grey and the gold on his sleeves was now almost the same colour as the light-brown dust that covered most of his fine jacket.

Lieutenant Simms took his Adams revolver from its holster and inspected it. He'd paid an exorbitant price for it in Washington and liked to brandish it. 'We're going to take a look over the hill, Sergeant,' he said, pointing with it. Then he replaced the gun in its holster and did not look down and admire it.

'Sir?'

'The Colonel was going to send cavalry, but I persuaded him that it was an infantry job.' The officer took off his campaign hat and wiped his face with a red kerchief. Winkelstein was surprised to notice that the Lieutenant was almost bald. It was strange that one could soldier with a man for nearly three months and then find out that he was almost bald. Winkelstein always thought of Lieutenant Simms as an impatient foolish child who would kill himself and all about him if someone did not temper his excitement with common sense. To discover that this child was bald came as a great surprise to Winkelstein. For once he allowed this emotion to register on his face.

Lieutenant Gideon Simms tried to guess what was in his Sergeant's mind. As always, he failed to guess. Simms suspected that the little German fellow had fought as a mercenary for the Confederates. Many such men had changed sides now that it was becoming clear that the South could not win. Simms did not fully trust the funny little German for that reason. On the other hand Sergeant

120

Winkelstein was the only senior NCO in the company who had had battle experience. Had the Colonel guessed that Winkelstein was a veteran, Simms would never have got him in the first place. Winkelstein also showed a businesslike way of keeping these stupid boys occupied to prevent them getting into mischief. And yet in some ways Simms would have preferred one of the other inexperienced men. Not only because he found it difficult to understand Winkelstein's thick accent but also because Winkelstein patronized him. It was nothing that he could put his finger on; nothing about which he could complain. Winkelstein did everything as well as it could be done and yet simply by so doing, he demonstrated that he should be wearing Simms's uniform. Simms's feeling of unease about Winkelstein found some relief in xenophobia, and to the other officers he made jokes about this little German who knew the drill book by heart and went to sleep at attention .

'*Lieutnant*!' said Winkelstein. 'Where are we to go?'

'Not you, Sergeant Winkelstein,' said Simms in a tone of weary sophistication. 'Four of your men.' Again he pointed. 'To the top of the hill, like the dear old Duke of York, don't yer know.'

Winkelstein knew nothing of the rhyme that told of ten thousand and one soldiers performing the motiveless antics that all armies did. He looked across to the hill that faced them. From there, one would be able to see all the way to the flat farmland into which the river ran from the valley. Winkelstein walked away as if to get a better view of the terrain and the Lieutcnant followed him. They both knew that the Sergeant wanted to be out of earshot of the soldiers. For a moment they watched two turkey vultures circling above the valley. From here they could look down upon them as they glided with only an occasional twitch of the wings. Their ugly red heads twisted as they sought a quarry.

'Why not send cavalry out of the valley?' Winkelstein pointed the way they should go.

'An hour there, an hour back,' explained the Lieutenant. 'Anyway, they wouldn't be able to see far from the end of the valley. A man on the hill there could see for twenty miles or more.'

'You want me not to go?' Winkelstein asked. He wanted to be quite certain of his military obligations.

'Send some of the farmers,' drawled Lieutenant Simms. 'Someone who can swim across the river if necessary: it might be deeper than it looks. They must make good time. I promised the colonel we'd tell him where the rebs were by noon.'

'Yes, sir.'

'And pick men with good boots,' said Simms. 'It's rough ground.'

'What if the enemy are already there?' asked Winkelstein.

Lieutenant Simms nodded. Winkelstein realized that Lieutenant Simms wasn't telling him the whole truth. All they wanted to know was whether the enemy were on that summit. Again Winkelstein took his binoculars and studied the hilltop and all the way down the slope as far as the stacked timber. He hoped that he would see a movement of grey uniforms, for then he would not have to send any of his men over there. Twenty minutes' hard walking to get there, twenty back. From the last of the trees there was no cover, all the way to the top. Winkelstein knew only two types of tree: those that gave cover and those that didn't. There was no place on the slopes that would provide a hiding-place for infantry under fire. Just one rifleman on the top could control the ground below him and kill as fast as he could reload. The same must obtain on the slope beyond the summit. So why send only a handful of men? Why not a company of

122

sharpshooters? Breechloaders up there could hold off the whole damned Confederate Army.

It took Sergeant Winkelstein almost three minutes to work out the conundrum. When he did, he cursed himself for a fool. If half a dozen infantrymen got to the hilltop alive then the colonel would put a cavalry troop over there. No. *Voll Idiot*, Winkelstein: artillery! The infantry were litmus paper to see if it was safe to put the artillery there. He looked again to the gun teams that had cantered past them five minutes ago. The first team were already in position in the shelter of a spur. From there they would be exposed for only half an hour before having their guns positioned and firing down the far slope.

'Green,' shouted Sergeant Winkelstein. 'Ashton, Harvey and Bray! Get your jackets on and pile your kit under the wagon.'

The rest of the company watched the four men as they hurried down into the valley and waded across the river. It was only knee deep.

'Now I know why Winkelstein didn't come,' Green said. 'He would have drowned.' The other three laughed. The sun was warm on their faces and the river reflected the light and cooled their aching feet. It made a pitter-pattering sound as the stones in its bed rolled gently in the currents. When they were all across the river Green waved to the line of infantry back at the top of the hill. He could just see the brown dots of their faces.

They put their socks and boots on to their wet feet and started up the far slope. It was harder going. They made a lot of noise as the metal studs of their boots slipped on the stony topsoil. Their progress was slow, and marked by clouds of dust. Ashton could smell the Georgia pines. They were different to the white pines they had in the North. In the hot sun these had a heady smell of resin hanging near them.

Ashton was last across the river, the others thirty yards

or so ahead of him. He didn't hurry; he was thinking about his last seven cigars. He didn't fancy giving three of them to Green, no matter about the socks or what he did to Sergeant Winkelstein. The pickets traded reb cigars for Union coffee. Now there was to be another battle, and it might be months before there came a chance to buy more. Perhaps he could get Green to agree that two cigars would be more appropriate. Ashton stood very still while he looked back at the river. It was clear enough for him to see the stony bottom. There would be fish there for certain. He'd seen a couple of kingfishers, and that was a sure sign. He could hear duck, too.

'C'mon, Josh. You wanna live for ever?' shouted Green from the rock at which he'd paused, flushed and sweaty from the exertions of his climb. Until that moment Ashton had never thought that he might be killed in the war. The possibility numbed him and made his heart beat disproportionately to his movements. He took the heavy Springfield in one hand and waved it in response, and was relieved when Green grinned and turned away to move up the hillside again.

This was no place for a man to give his life. This fight would not be in the history books or dignified as a battle honour. Only bereaved mothers and pining sweethearts would remember this encounter, and they would probably get the name wrong. What place was it? This valley had no name, and there were no newspaper men here to name it 'Bloody Ridge' or 'Bald Mountain' or 'Death Valley'. And what newspapermen didn't see, never happened.

Nor was this a fitting time to die. Soon the army would retire into winter quarters, or so the rumour went. They might be cold or hungry but they'd not be shot at until spring. A whole winter of life.

From the top of the hill the company watched the four men. This was the first time they had been close to the war. Winkelstein didn't tell them to continue digging. He'd not seen them stop, for his binoculars were focused on the hilltop and held tight to his eyes. As the men fell silent the sounds of the countryside intruded. There were flies and wasps attracted to the dead horse which was bloated and stinking, a soft, obscene, unrecognizable shape half buried in the weed-filled ditch. Insects buzzing in the grass made a sound like the telegraph wires that followed the railroad tracks across the continent. There were birds singing, too.

Winkelstein did not take the field glasses from his eyes. He saw the grey uniforms long before the four soldiers could see them. Winkelstein stared through the glasses: plain-topped kepis – probably infantry. The red of the artillery or the yellow of the cavalry would have been visible through his binoculars.

Soon a sharp-eyed farm boy saw that the rebs were there. 'Jesus! They are walking on to them!'

'They can't see them.'

'Shall we whistle?' He was a friend of Joshua Ashton.

'You will be silent,' said Winkelstein, but then relented. 'Whistle if you want, but they will not hear. The wind is the other way.'

The boy whistled but Winkelstein was right. The sound did not carry to the far slope.

'They're letting them get close to take them prisoner,' said Ashton's friend.

'No,' said Winkelstein. 'They want the boots. The rebs are short of boots.'

They saw the smoke long seconds before they heard the faint sound of the shots. Joshua Ashton went down first. He was on a steep incline and he went down head over heels all the way to the pines. He inhaled their scent, clawed at their roots and bled into the mouldy earth.

Green was the only one who lived long enough to

return the rifle-fire. Kneeling behind a rock he fired twice. It was mere bravado: he couldn't see the Confederate infantry above him. It would be only a matter of minutes before they found him. Green shifted round so that his back was against the boulder. From here he could see the men of his company, Winkelstein was so much shorter than the others. He watched as Winkelstein gave the order to dig the ditch deeper. Every man in the company stripped off his coat and put every ounce of energy into his task. No one sniggered at Winkelstein's accent or gave him cause for displeasure.

Mission Control: Hannibal One

All night I had been inside my headquarters, listening to the wind playing demented tunes upon the army badges, eagles and other paraphernalia that a publicity-conscious army commander had provided to mark the progress of our tiny expedition. I dressed myself in my heavy clothing before venturing outside. The wind blew with renewed violence as I emerged through the shelter's small flap. Each gust crooned a low warning that seemed to vibrate the whole planet before becoming the shrill complaining shriek that penetrated to the centre of my brain. It was a feat of willpower to think clearly. But I was the Mission Commander; unless I was able to think clearly, we might all die.

Others had been here, but only for a few hours at a time. We were the first soldiers to come, and now it looked as if we would be the first men to wage war here. It was a terrible place to fight a battle: a fatal place to lose it. It was a bleak, barren, metallic landscape like none other I had ever seen. I looked up through the clear air, and recognized the constellation of Pleiades, now setting. The neighbouring stars were growing dim. I remembered how as a child I had dreamed of travelling to them.

My second-in-command was an engineer. He was a balding veteran of many years. A fierce disciplinarian with his subordinates, even I was not immune from his scarcastic jeers about youth and inexperience. Perhaps that's why one of the southerners dealing out the rations that day decided to complain directly to me.

'This clothing isn't warm enough, sir. I didn't know it would be as cold as this.'

'You're wearing the same as the others,' I said. 'You'd be no use to the army in a cocoon.'

'It's such a poor-quality material the cold wind goes right through it,' he said, examining his white tunic with finger and thumb. 'A profiteer with an army contract and friends in the Senate doesn't have to worry about how cold we feel.'

'That's all, soldier,' I told him. I wasn't going to let these 'boots' think that the informality that prevailed on these missions extended to the priviledge of sedition. 'You volunteered for the trip and your application was endorsed by your CO and agreed by me. Did we all make a mistake about you, soldier?'

'No, sir,' he yelled. 'It's just that where I come from, in the south,' he smiled, because his accent made the qualification unnecessary, 'we never knew temperatures like this.'

I looked at him. He was a weak-faced kid. He'd cut himself shaving, and a spider of dried blood crawled down his jawline. He was probably a good enough soldier left to do a soldier's job, but here he felt inadequate, and those were the ones who showed fear first.

'I'm not looking forward to the trip back, sir. And now the men say there will be fighting before we return.'

There had been mistakes and emergencies during the ascent. The boy needed reassurance. 'It's a routine mission. It was a thousand-to-one chance that they would have men up here, too.' It was a lie, but it seemed to do the trick for him.

'There's no doubt about them being here, then?'

'They're not local inhabitants, if that's what you mean,' I said rather brutally. I spoke too loud, I suppose. My second-in-command heard me and chortled. He looked foward to the fighting. For two decades he'd been in

128

every war the army had fought and he knew that it was the quickest way to promotion. I kept my eyes on the youngster. 'Our mission is reconnaissance, but if they come into this area we will oppose their transit. If that means fighting, we fight.' I saw my Second nod. He turned towards us; he couldn't keep out of a conversation like this. He prodded the boy with enough force to make him wince.

'If you don't like it up here, go home,' he jeered.

The boy flushed. That summed it up, really; no one could get back alone, so there was nothing to discuss. The boy turned to go, but he gripped him by the arm.

'Listen, boot, did you wonder what those apes are doing up here? You think they came here to enjoy the view? OK. Well, if they keep to their side of that,' he pointed vaguely to the ugly outcrops of rock ahead of us, 'then no one will worry them. If they poke their dirty faces around the side of it . . .' He snapped his fingers in a way that left no doubt that it would be an easy fight. Perhaps that was the best way of reassuring the boy. And of reassuring them all.

I said, 'We think they are here for strategic reasons. From here they can launch an attack that would raze our cities and decimate our women and children. They will have machines with them . . . Well, you will see.'

'Now get going on the ration detail,' said the Second, and followed him to be sure that it was done satisfactorily.

When they had gone, I went to stare again at the landscape. The sun's orbit brought it over the peaks behind us. In this clear air the light was redder than I'd ever seen, and I watched the strange terrain change from blue to pink. It seemed odd that my wife would see this same fiery planet and rejoice in its warmth as it brought another dawn for our people at home. As I watched the pink light spill into the valleys and crevasses I heard the sounds of the main unit awakening. Even before reveille ended I could hear the metallic clink of weapon checks. They were good men: uncomplaining and loyal. I hoped that the events of the day would not cause me to change my opinion of them.

There was still another wheatcake left with my breakfast. I gobbled it hastily, knowing that I might not eat again for some time. I removed my helmet and wiped the sweat from my close-cropped head, hearing the sentries change with a lot of ceremony and feet-stamping, and then finally my second-in-command brought the parade to attention and reported to me, 'Special Mission One: on duty, sir.'

I returned his salute with parade-ground precision. Already the blood had drained out of the sun, and there was no heat in it. An icy wind bit into me as I walked down the silent ranks of soldiers. I could see from their expressions that they longed to get their circulation moving again. I noticed too how grimy their clothing had become in the short time. There were no laundry facilities here, so I could not reprimand a man for a dirty uniform. And yet such things – as those who had served under me before well knew – were an important part of my theories of discipline.

'At ease, soldiers,' I shouted. They looked at me quizzically. It was an unusual form of address: soldiers are seldom called soldiers by soldiers, just as artists are never called artists by their fellow artists. I waited until the first strenuous efforts to keep warm were over and then continued. 'Soldiers, today you will make history that your children will read. Your children's children, perhaps, will remember your part in the history of our great nation. Free men will always be called upon to make sacrifices that freedom may survive. Some of my senior soldiers will remember other battles in Germany, France and North Africa, where their comrades died in order that the younger men among you could grow up in freedom. Now you in turn are asked to do the same. We will prove true to that trust in us.' It was going well, damned well. I had their attention; they had even to some extent forgotten the cold. 'You are a part of the finest, best-equipped and most scientific army that the world has ever seen. We were not sent here to fight, but we brought weapons with us because the Government knew that these people who use the word "peace" so often, who profess to bring brotherhood and prosperity to the whole world, have nothing but hatred and envy in their hearts.'

I paused, casually fingering the screaming eagles on my tunic. 'The Commander-in-Chief has asked the Senate to rush a Task Force to our support. Until they get here the eyes of the world are upon us.' These high-flown words held them rapt for a moment while I issued a rapid series of orders. 'Communications detail: report to your officer for special instructions. Special duty men: stand fast. Kitchen detail: break camp. Advance party: formate to move north under commander's orders. All remaining personnel: on parade with weapons and entrenchment tools in five minutes. Parade: to your duties. Dis-miss!'

They broke up and doubled away faster than ever before. The urgent attention to detail would drive all anxieties from their minds. My Second ambled across to me with the insolence that a fine combat record permitted. He undid the strap of his helmet and dropped it to the ground. It angered me that he should thus treat an expensive piece of equipment while standing before me. He said, 'You think all that stuff does them any good?'

'Don't you?' I asked haughtily.

'Not a hope. But if it makes you feel better, OK.' He took out a flask and gulped a mouthful. 'They don't believe that crap any more than you do.' He offered me the flask. I was very angry, and for a moment I wanted to remind him of my seniority and have him standing rigidly to attention and shouting affirmative monosyllables like a recruit. He must have read my mind, for he shook his head slowly and said, 'No, it's too late for that.'

I nodded, accepting the flask, and took a long drink. I should have done that hours before. I pulled a face as it tore a warm furrow through the cold, soft earth of my gut.

'They know,' he said.

'They know what?'

He sighed. 'They know that our mission wasn't publicized. A couple of Senators may know we are here, but the last thing they are going to do is send a Task Force after us. I liked that "Communications detail: report to your officer for special instructions" . . .' He mimicked my accent, making the slight Neapolitan consonants that I had inherited from my father into a street-vendor's cry, all the words linked into a sing-song chant. He nodded. 'That might shore up your story for ten minutes, but those Communications boots are the biggest loudmouths in the army. That's way they go for that job. Special instructions!' He laughed. 'Special instructions . . .' It seemed to amuse him that I had chosen those words.

'I suppose we both expected it to be like this?' I said.

'I read the entrails,' he replied. 'I've always said that we should have kept going on those babies two decades ago. Instead, the politicians put our name on a peace treaty with them.' He paused. 'I hate those bastards.'

'There's too much to do to waste time hating half the world,' I said. 'Too much to build, to mend, to discover. We should have been working together all this time, instead of the two halves of the world rattling swords at each other.'

He spat, and swore.

'You've seen combat,' I argued. 'You've seen what a modern army can do. How can you want to fight?' I shivered. 'Aren't the elements enemy enough? We still know too little about the world we live in.'

'You should have been a doctor or a lawyer or an artist or something. By jupiter, I'll wait until you've seen these barbarians for yourself. I'll wait until you've seen what they do with our prisoners. Cruelty is part of their official policy, just as lying is. They have no religion; nothing is sacred to them. There are no standards that we have in common with these bastards. Sooner or later you'll have to face the fact that violence is the only language they understand.'

'I've seen some combat,' I said distantly. He smiled the cold sad smile that he kept for recruits who said something especially foolish. We both knew that I had been chosen for this command because of my brilliant scholastic record, and that he was there to provide the blunter skills of the combat engineer. But the tactics of bridging rivers under fire wasn't going to help us now, any more than my theoretical science.

'Believe me, sir,' he said, 'riot control in our cities, police actions against guerrillas or some tiny satellite nation on the far side of the world is one thing, this is another. We are going to come face to face with the finest soldiers they can select. They'll have modern weapons and good leadership. I don't think we'll be able to stop them.'

I'd never heard him talk like this. I realized that his brash and belligerent manner concealed a dark despair.

'They're not supermen,' I said with a smile. 'They're just a mixture of nationalities from every corner of the world.'

'Like us?' he smiled.

'Exactly.' He was always talking about race and nationality, which made me wonder what his own origins were: German, perhaps.

The scream cut through the air like a spurt of blood. Three of our men, their uniforms mud-spattered and torn, were running as fast as Olympic champions. Behind them there was a fourth. He was holding his side as he ran, leaving a trail of red spots, each one bigger than the last. The whole unit broke formation as the three men of the advance party ran past them without even a glance at their comrades. The fourth man was level with me now, and I stepped out to stand in his path. He stopped. His eyes were huge and full of tears. 'You said they were men!' he accused. 'You said we'd be fighting *men*!' His voice was shrill to the point of hysteria. His helmet was askew, but the spider of blood on his jaw told me that it was the boy I'd spoken with. I grabbed his arm but he broke away from me with a surprising force. I looked down and found that my tunic was smeared with fresh shiny blood from the youngster's wounds. I watched him as he followed the others down a steep incline, dodging between the rocky outcrops. 'Come back!' I shouted. The wind snatched my voice away. I cupped my hands round my mouth. 'Come back at once! I'll have you executed!'

It was no use. The rest of them had sniffed the scent of panic and were scrambling down the hillside too. Only a few of the hardiest old campaigners remained in the roadway looking the way the four men had come. For a moment I had hope, but then they saw the sight that the others had seen and they too gibbered with fear.

'Don't be afraid,' I said, 'don't be afraid. I've seen them before. They are large, but they are controlled by men no better than us.'

Two of my senior sergeants then prostrated themselves on the roadway, screaming a mixture of prayers and oaths that betrayed a mankind for whom witchcraft lay just under the skin of science.

Other soldiers were ripping their hands and legs on the rocks and stony ledges below me as they half-ran and half-fell towards the sheltered basin in which we had camped the previous night. 'Alive!' my soldiers were shouting. 'They are alive! They are alive!'

They would not escape. There was no escape from here. Already some of the men who had fallen were not able to regain their feet. A thousand feet below me were men who could have got there only by throwing themselves bodily from the narrow crevasse. Wearily, I turned back to where my second-in-command was standing. He'd not moved.

'Who could have believed it?' I asked, as I stood there with the bald officer: just two of us between the invaders and the rich, lush land of Italy. 'Who could have believed that Hannibal would bring elephants over the Alps?'

Adagio

Flying Officer Woodhall put a hand to the gunsight and switched it on. A circle glowed orange in the centre of his bullet-proof windscreen. He adjusted the sight, narrowing the bars to the correct setting for a Heinkel 111. Woodhall was a Cranwell man, professional pilot and regular officer. He'd commanded B Flight since the beginning of July when David disappeared during a mix-up over the Estuary. The rest of his flight were tight behind him: a vic three, and then another vic three – red section – led by 'Happy' Hogg. It was a stupid formation with which to attack enemy bombers. Only the silly bastards at the Air Ministry could have invented such a pattern. It probably looked rather good as a coloured diagram on a sheet of card. Already some squadrons – auxiliary squadrons, he suspected – had unofficially abandoned the vic. They were doing it like the Huns: pairs in sections of four. *Rotte*, the Huns called the pair. Flying like that you could weave constantly, looking over your shoulder to make sure you were not about to be bounced. Some of the pilots had still not got into the habit of looking over their shoulder. In the Gauntlet open-cockpit biplanes that they had so recently flown it has been a certain way of losing your goggles in the slipstream. Woodhall glanced at the tiny mirror. He could see the other section following him. Woodhall might try the new formation next week, if he survived, but disobeying even stupid orders did not come easily to Cranwell men.

His hands moved to the microphone on his face mask and switched it on. 'Blue leader here. Tally ho! I've got them, about fifty bandits: heavy jobs, Heinkel one one ones. Vector three five five . . .'

The Hurricane was a good climber, but on the straight and level it was slow. Obviously one should get above the bogeys and come out of the sun, but if one spent too much time manoeuvring the Huns might bomb before being attacked. Group got very nasty when that happened. David got a stupendous rocket when three Dorniers plastered Manston, even though they had put paid to all three within a couple of minutes.

Just a shade more up-sun. There was no ground target worth bombing under their track. He looked at the map on his knee, running his finger under the expected path of the bombers. The second finger of his glove was chewed at the tip where he always pulled it off with his teeth. He looked at the left-hand glove; it was exactly the same. He turned his hand to see the gold watch that he wore on the inner side of the wrist: 12.15 precisely. Forty-five minutes until lunchtime. Fuel for another thirty-five minutes. At a rough guess, three runs through this mob before their fighter escort mix it. Then five minutes' grab-arse with the 109s, and home-james, with enough juice to stooge across to the satellite field if they've done it on the doorstep meanwhile.

The Hurricane was inferior to the Messerschmitt Bf 109, and that was no secret that must be guarded from the enemy. That's why the controllers sent Hurricane squadrons to intercept the bombers while the Spitfires climbed and climbed towards the fighters that waited up there at thirty thousand feet, stacked up like rush-hour crowds on a vast moving staircase.

Flying Officer Woodhall turned the safety ring to 'fire' and let his eyes relax to provide him with a view through the sight, as well as glimpse the lumbering formation of Heinkels at which he was now flying at something not too far removed from 400 mph. The ugly great bombers sailed on, indifferent to any interruption. He inched the stick forward and as usual heard the carburettors miss a pulse-beat as the centrifugal force starved them of fuel.

Only the new boys complained of having no time, just as inexperienced drivers could never find the time to change gear. For Woodhall there was never a hurry. Always as the formations rushed together time slowed. Now, every inch of forward movement seemed to take two or three minutes. He had enough time to look left and see the curve of the Kentish coast lost in a grey mist near Margate. Beyond it the sea sparkled in the sunlight, as warm and inviting as the railway posters always portrayed it. High above, the enemy's fighter escort had not even begun to turn. Unless they did so soon, the Spitfires would have enough height to come out of the sun at them. The Spitfire formations were up on the horizon, and given that fixed point Woodhall could persuade himself that they were the only moving component of this transfixed world.

Hours ago he had chosen which one of them was to be his. The angle of the dive would already have confirmed it to the others, and each of them would now be choosing one of the plump green whales for himself. Woodhall would have the leader. He always attacked the leader. That gave the others maximum room for manoeuvre in lining up their own victims. He looked at his instruments: oil pressure and temperature, boost, revs, turn and bank, air-speed, altitude. It was idle curiosity, really; he knew the Hurricane was behaving perfectly. If any of the clocks had shown any reading but the one he expected it would have meant that the instrument was faulty. It would simply be something to report to his basher after landing. His hand was resting on the throttle. He moved it. He wouldn't throttle back until they were way out the other side and reforming. These gloves had been very good. His mother had bought them for him when he got his wings. What was that, 'thirty-seven? No, earlier; nineteen thirty-six. My God, how time passed sometimes. Going at the fingertips. His gloves always went there; perhaps his fingers were longer than average. He must stop that habit of tugging the fingertips, for that would split any gloves, even a pair like this from Harrods. That was nerves.

Damn well made, these Heinkels. He could see every rivet on this one. They weren't as hastily put in as the rivets on his own aircraft. He looked out to see the riveting on his own mainplane. Just as he'd remembered, there was a line of them unevenly placed with a couple of extra ones punched to one side.

To his left he could see Sergeant Patch. He was the fat boy of the squadron. No Mess charges in the Sergeants' Mess and the food was almost exactly the same as the officers'. Better, sometimes; they'd got on to some black-market johnny who let them have things cheaply. Con-science, probably. It was miraculous how Patch fitted into the narrow pilot seat. Woodhall was slim and there was scarcely enough room for him to twist his bottom when he got cramp. He moved his weight now. The metal buckles of his parachute harness bit into a thigh. Better perhaps to be Patch and be self-upholstered. He could see the fierce concentration of Patch in spite of the goggles and face mask. The set of his shoulders was exactly as it was during the poker games in the dispersal hut. Woodhall grinned. There was no chance of attracting the Sergeant's attention now. Nothing existed for Serge-ant Patch except his gunsight inside which the enemy bomber was expanding almost too fast for Patch to calculate the deflection.

Woodhall saw the ailerons move on the Heinkel to the left of him. There was a hesitation before the airflow took effect upon the altered aerofoil. Then the wing lifted and the pilot corrected as the bomber nosed in tighter to its leader like a frightened animal. Woodhall felt hot under the rubber face mask. He unclipped the mask, and knocked his nose with the back of his gloved hand. It was another nervous habit. They all had them. They were all tired. The day before yesterday – Woodhall wasn't sure whether that would be Tuesday or Wednesday – A-Flight commander had taxied to the dispersal and made no attempt to even slide back the cover or open the flap-door. They all thought he was badly shot up. Woodhall feared he would be dead – Baxter was a bloody good bloke, the last of the Cranwell chaps in the Squadron – but when they got there, Baxter wasn't dead. Baxter was sound asleep.

The Spitfires were above the skyline now. Except for a straggler who was falling farther and farther behind. Carburettor, probably; even the Spits still had carburettors. The Bf 109 had fuel injection. You could throw those crates around the sky without a hiccup. All the Heinkels were drawing closer together. As they did so they wallowed in the air like a convoy on a heavy sea. The AA guns still hadn't stopped firing. In a clear piece of air in front of Woodhall's Heinkel a yellow flash turned orange. Then its centre became red and the air rippled with a shock wave and distorted the neat green fields. A thin film of dust formed behind the shock wave and built up particle upon particle until a soft billowing cloud of smoke was cut in two by the Heinkel's wing. The Heinkel had buffeted fiercely. The pilot was fighting the controls. The upper Rear Gunner released his grip on the machine-gun and grabbed at the Perspex edge of his screen. The nose gun tilted too, and Woodhall guessed that its gunner had been thrown into a heap by the sudden movement.

Woodhall could picture the pilot. Leading a formation of this size would be a Major or even an Oberstleutnant. A tough old bastard with a tic at his eye and highly polished top-boots. Woodhall had seen such a man under escort at Waterloo Station last month.

The Hurricanes were flattening the curve of their attack. Each passing second Woodhall moved the stick the merest fraction back. Here comes the shock wave, he thought, as the control column put pressure upon his hand and made him tense his wrist until it was Indian-wrestling with him. Suddenly the pressure was gone, so that his stick fell forward – or would have, if he had not been prepared for the shock wave to pass as abruptly as it had come.

For the third time in the last twelve seconds Woodhall pressed the throttle. It was as far forward as it could go. Again he noticed his glove. Again he pressed it against his nose. This time however he reclipped his face mask. It had been open for only as much time as it took him to run the tip of his tongue along his dry lips.

High above them in the dome of the sky, where it was at its bluest, a dozen tiny scratches crawled towards the Messerschmitts. The Spitfires had gone too high in trying to get above the fighter escort. Now they would be spotted. The Messerschmitts had not changed their course by even a fraction of a degree. Within seconds they must decide whether to turn and face the Spitfires or come down here and get into the brawl.

'. . . I'll take the leader, Happy take the bugger with the coloured tail.' Woodhall finished the message. It seemed so long ago that he'd begun to speak that he scarcely remembered the whole thing. Yet the others had scarcely noticed the pause as he wet his lips. He corrected the rudder and took another look at Sergeant Patch. Then he said, 'Out,' to complete the message and switched the microphone off. The speed was making the Hurricane vibrate, and even through his flying boots he felt the rudder bar shuddering.

In the earphones he heard Happy say, 'The guns,

Christ, the guns!' and could scarcely believe that it had taken the others so long to see the explosion. The length of their reaction time worried him. It was like being behind some driver at the traffic lights and waiting ages before he reacted to the green. Already ahead of the Heinkel he could see the faint yellowish sparkle that was the beginning of another explosion. The gun's predictor was working well today. '. . . they are firing, Woody.' The voice was deep and wobbly, like a recording played at the wrong speed.

In June, Winston had said that the Battle of Britain was about to begin. Had he meant an invasion, or had he meant this fighting in the air? Already some of the BBC chaps were talking about the RAF fighting the Battle of Britain. The other night in the Mess, even the old station master had used the same expression. Mind you, it wasn't the sort of thing one would say in front of civvies. It would seem too much like line-shooting. But here alone up in the sky, moving on to this formation of Heinkels as fast as they could go, it was perhaps permissible to think of himself as a warrior taking part in a mighty battle. A battle as wide as England and as high as the stratosphere, a battle like no other in the history of the world: the Battle of Britain.

'. . . Over,' said Happy. Well, that meant he was expecting some sort of reply. The gunfire had alarmed him because it was unexpected. It was not on orders. He was a good fellow – Pilot Officer Happy Hogg – and he was in for a gong: two Dorniers in one day as well as half a Stuka the month before. There were no more Stukas coming this way nowadays. What would a chap do if he found himself fighting a war in a Stuka or a Defiant or a Blenheim? What chance did any of those chaps stand up against a modern plane? The Hurribird was inferior to the Spit, but only by a narrow margin, and it had a couple of advantages, too. But those Stukas were a catastrophe looking for a convenient place to occur. In a way, these bomber johnnies were in the same position. Who'd want to fight a war piloting a barge like that. Or even worse, as a gunner or an observer in it, not even the master of one's own fate. That was Woodhall's idea of purgatory. His parents could never see it like that. They couldn't see that a fighter pilot is privileged to fight in his own way.

Woodhall reached again to his microphone. The second anti-aircraft shell was a jagged red flash. 'Blue Leader here . . .' He really must cut out this affected drawl he'd acquired from Baxter. It was bad R/T procedure for one thing, and some of the chaps found it irritating. Yesterday he'd heard his rigger say, 'Here comes Lord Haw-Haw.' It wasn't meant in any spiteful way, but it had decided him to do something about it. He made his voice higher and brisk. '. . . the gunfire is friendly, chaps. Don't be fright,' he chided them. He saw Sergeant Patch turn to look at him and knew he would be giving a girlish giggle. The flash turned to smoke and floated past the Heinkel but this time the shock wave affected neither aircraft. '. . . Out.'

The Heinkel had been in the upper section of his cockpit cover but now it was oozing into the toughened glass. Its Rear Upper Gunner brought his machine-gun round. It twisted as the barrel poked out into the violent slipstream. The Heinkel on the left – Sergeant Patch's target – began to fire. The tracers curved away before they were anywhere near Patch. He was nervous, that Gunner. Not so the fellow who was creeping towards Woodhall's optical sight. The leader was bound to have the finest crewmen he could get. In the same way Woodhall kept Sergeant Patch as his wingman. He wasn't an imaginative fellow but he'd chalked up nine hundred hours and he'd hang on like grim death. If Woodhall flew through a railway tunnel, Patch would still be wing-tip to wing-tip as they came out the other end.

Woodhall made the slightest of corrections to his line of flight. The others would be all tight against him. If he flew in with the correct deflection then there was a good chance that the others would have theirs correct, too. The body of the Heinkel moved round the gunsight rings like the sweep-second hand of a watch: enough. He corrected and held it steady.

The deflection was right, now he had only to wait while the Heinkel got bigger in his gunsight. The waiting was the worst part of it. If the airspeed needle wasn't fixed at 380 mph Woodhall could have believed that the Heinkel was towing him.

He remembered a joke about the theory of relativity: a chap spending three minutes in a dentist's chair thinks it's an hour. A chap spending an hour in bed with the blonde WAAF from Met thinks it's three minutes. The punch line was something about – And for this they made this bloke Einstein a professor! When you come to think about it, the fact behind the joke is that time goes slower when you hate what's happening. Well, Woodhall didn't hate this combat, nor did he have the pain that he'd felt in a dentist's chair, and yet the time crept past as slowly as in a nightmare. It was then Woodhall decided that the slowness was fear. How curious that he had never realized that before. Someone had described a bad motor-car accident as all happening in slow motion. They too had been afraid without knowing it. The Doc was an interesting chap; perhaps he'd take it up with him. My God, no! If he said anything like that to a quack they'd think it was the first sign of a crack-up. Perhaps it *was* the first sign of a crack-up. They all knew that opening fire too early was something that newly arrived sprogs did. But it was also a thing that chaps did when they were overtired. Baxter opened fire too soon on Monday. No, tell a lie: Tuesday,

144

it was, with Dorniers at Gravesend. This gunner shooting at Patch might be scared. The reasoning was that a chap could get everything over more quickly if one opened fire. Fallacious reasoning, but it was easy to see how it might seem correct.

Ah, now Woodhall's fellow was having a go. Yes, he was giving him a squirt. The Heinkels were so close together that they had no room for jinking. Two more anti-aircraft shells over on the port side of the formation, but no one was hit. The Messerschmitts had finally made up their mind: they were turning back to have a go at the Spitfires. Good. That meant that Woodhall and his chaps might get three passes at the Heinkels before the 109s got to them. Funny how 109s always did that half-roll and vertical dive. They must teach them that at their training schools. There they go: a perfect plan-view as they tipped over. Woodhall decided that his next pass would be a head-on. Then he could do a stern attack for the third one and be pointing in the general direction of base for a quick get-away.

The gunner in Woodhall's Heinkel was good, just as he'd guessed he would be. He was aiming high so that Woodhall must fly into it. Not like Patch's fellow. His tracer was curving under the Hurricane and falling short. That was really stupid because the deflection was decreasing all the time. Unless the gunner made a big correction – with all the chances of going too far over the target – he'd fire short through the whole attack.

When Patch opened fire, Woodhall could still see the two aeroplanes out of the corner of his eye. The Hurricane's eight guns converged upon the Heinkel like fine silver wires down which the Hurricane slid. Or more accurately, thought Woodhall, as though the wires were drawing the two aeroplanes together. Patch's two port outer guns were misaligned. The armourers had lined them up to fire straight ahead. Most of the squadron's guns were mounted like that, but for chaps like Patch and Baxter and Woodhall – chaps who knew their ranges and got in close – the guns were mounted to converge. Woodhall would speak to the armament officer about that. It could make all the difference to a kill. It wouldn't make much difference to this one, though. The gunner had gone already and the machine-gun fire was ploughing a furrow through the fuselage, ripping the soft metal open like a can-opener.

Woodhall glanced around the cockpit before fixing his eye upon the optical sight. Everything was as it should be. The Heinkel was trapped inside the concentric rings like a fly struggling in a web. Gently he pushed the gun button. It was like hitting a jelly at high speed. The guns rattled his teeth. The nose dipped – it always did – and Woodhall corrected for it. The airspeed dropped by 38 mph.

'Oh, my God!' said Woodhall. Actually he didn't put the exclamation mark in. He said it in the bored and unhurried voice that he used when he accepted his bar bills. A man who spends all his time around aeroplanes acquires the knack of knowing what they are going to do. It's the way they sit in the air and also the way they are handled and the smoothness with which they change direction. Or, as in this case, the way they didn't change direction. He had clearly said that it was going to be a stern attack passing over the enemy formation. He only went right through an enemy formation when they had a fighter escort in close attendance. The few times he had done it the whole flight were all over the place, and instead of pulling up tight underneath the bombers to conserve height they left far too much safety margin. But Patch of all people . . . it was too bad.

Woodhall switched the microphone on, steering and firing with one hand. 'Patch – ' was all he had time to say before the port wing of Patch's Hurricane chopped right

146

through the starboard wing of the Heinkel he was attacking. The Hurricane wing was scarcely damaged by the impact. That could be expected; it was the basis of party tricks in which tiresome uncles broke walking-sticks without damaging wine-glasses. The Heinkel wing twisted away without breaking off. It was like the flapping wing of a gull suddenly bored with gliding, but this gull was leaving a trail of feathers. The propeller broke up and then the aeroplane tilted over like a . . . Like a what, thought Woodhall, still looking at it. Not like a gull, more like a harpooned whale snorting salt spray, spouting bubbles and turning its nose in demented pain and screaming in terror. Now that it was a whale, Woodhall felt more compassion for it than he had for the manned machine. Poor Huns, poor bloody Huns.

And poor Patch. He had bought it. Woodhall didn't look that way. Jesus, poor Patch! Patch had giggled. Patch was an ex-brat with over 900 hours on Spits. Patch was in for a DFM. Patch couldn't get drunk, even when he tried. Patch owed Happy ten pounds which Happy would never see and badly needed. Patch had a mother who lived in Portsmouth and Patch couldn't decide whether to make her go and stay with her sister in Leeds. Patch was the worst goalie Woodhall had ever seen but the Wingco just wouldn't boot him out of the team. Patch had the new-style flying-boots. That was everything that Woodhall knew about Patch.

His own target was taking a pasting. Each bullet burned a big silver coin in the paintwork so that the bomber seemed to be showered with newly minted half-crowns. All over the fuselage they stuck, appearing like magic pox upon the wings and the port-engine cowling until the engine hid itself in a white cloud of coolant. Break now, Woodhall told himself. He took his finger off the button, the intricate cat's-cradle snapped and the two aeroplanes separated. The disc that had been the Heinkel's revolving

147

propeller blades went dark on one side where the engine was suffering friction. Unless they feathered immediately the prop would break up.

As Woodhall's Hurricane passed over the Heinkel he could feel the closeness of the other plane. Perhaps it was the sound, or a change in the reflected light or the pressure of the air, but whatever it was it gave Woodhall a curious feeling of being one with the machine. Patch must have copped it during the dive. It just wasn't Patch's style to ram the brute, so he must have been unconscious or crippled and unable to move. It happens. We all know it happens. Poor Patch. Woodhall began to compose the letter to Patch's mother. He'd written three in the last ten days so he knew the form by now. If only the relatives knew what it took out of a chap to write a next-of-kin letter they would make do with the Air Ministry telegram. Perhaps Patch had left a last letter. Now that was very much in character. He was a good chap: self-conscious and shy and keen to give no one any trouble. Woodhall would still mention that misalignment of the guns to the armament bod. Some of the pilots had their guns loaded with every other bullet a De Wilde instead of one in five. The armourers objected because the incendiary bullets fouled the guns, but it might be worth trying. It would be politic to mention that at the same time.

Above them the Messerschmitts and Spitfires were now only a mile apart. Woodhall fixed a point in the sky to which he would bring the Flight for a head-on attack. He looked around. They were all with him, but the two new pilots were strung out a bit. A gentle curve to port would give them a chance to cut the corner and catch up. Woodhall liked them in tight behind him. There was no need to tell them on the blower. They'd soon get the idea.

Woodhall brought the stick over before putting on any rudder. It gave them a chance to get into the turn as soon

148

as he did. One day before the war he'd flown in a formation of Gauntlets. They were all thousand-hour chaps and the formation leader didn't have to do anything like that. They were tight in behind him no matter what he did. Woodhall would love to lead such men in a high-speed monoplane formation. No babying anyone, no R/T warnings, no banks before turning, everyone's reaction time as fast as his own. Faster perhaps.

He looked down towards the tilting earth. The mist parted, and for a moment there was revealed a grand design of fields and villages, linked by roads both straight and crooked, beset by pits and surmounted with peaks. The world turned grey once more. With such brief clarity must a man find God.

Now some rudder. One silly sod hadn't even started yet. Great Scot! What did these fellows do when they were flying? Did they never see anything? The two new bods were catching up. That's good, he didn't want to throttle back to wait for them. The first of the 109s had broken formation to get at the Spits. Funny, that, he would have kept them together. Some Staff bugger along for the ride, trying to chalk up a kill to impress the brass-hats. Last month they'd had a chap from Group tag along with them in a Spitfire. They'd had a bundle with some 109s and the poor old sod had bought it. Woodhall knew exactly what had happened: a Hurricane had shot it down. A Spit can look very like a Bf 109 in front elevation – and that's the view you get when you've got to make the fastest decision. Anyway, a chap flying a Hurribird in a mêlée is awfully tempted to shoot at anything that doesn't look like a Hurribird. Of course, Woodhall had never uttered these thoughts.

They were tight together again now. The Heinkels were keeping a steady course. 'Blue Leader to Blue and Red sections. Line astern: go! Head-on. We'll go under them but don't lose height. Out.' After he switched the microphone off Woodhall snorted to himself: these line-astern formations were another RAF absurdity. Woodhall looked in his mirror. The Heinkel Patch had hit was miles away; a great trail of smoke jabbing into the mist. No parachutes anywhere.

Two more of the Heinkels were crippled. Both were doing all they could to keep formation but they were beginning to slide back through it. The leader was also losing height. When they had gone through the formation again Woodhall would have to decide whether to go after the stragglers or try again to break up the formation. He shouldn't really have to make the decision, his orders were quite clear, but it wasn't easy to leave two like that so that some sprog has only to follow them until they crash in order to claim a kill. Oh well, he mustn't become victory-happy. That was just for the VR chaps and the fellows from the auxiliary squadrons. Regulars are paid to be airmen. They are paid to stay at the sharp end, obeying the stupid orders as well as the clever ones. Regulars fly in proper uniform with collar and tie and with life jacket tied. If the others wanted to fly in shirtsleeves and civvy cardigans, do victory rolls and get their photos in the newspapers, well, that was all right too.

Woodhall tapped the throttle and unclipped the face mask to scratch the side of his nose. Even through his glove he could feel that his face was wet with perspiration. He reclipped the mask and stole a glance at his wrist-watch. It was 12.16. Forty-four minutes to go until lunch. In that minute he'd travelled nearly seven miles.

The two crippled Heinkels were both losing height now. Perhaps he'd let one of the boys claim half of his. On the other hand, would that imbue the boy with a false confidence and make him do something stupid? Oh well, he'd have plenty of opportunity for making that decision during the next attack.

Bonus for a Salesman

My dear old friend,

Public relations or not, Perce, it's still nice of you to remember my birthday, and thank you for the new catalogue. When you retire next month there will be no one at the firm who was there in my time. I hope you can read my writing, Percy. As you well know, I was never good at writing letters or any other sort of paperwork which is, I suppose, why I wanted to get out on the road instead of staying inside that miserable little office in Railway Street. On that last trip though, the girl did it all for me. Perhaps you noticed the good handwriting.

The girl, I had picked up in Caracas or Trinidad or somewhere up there in the north, so it must have been soon after the trip began. I always worked south to Rio and then came back across the South Atlantic in a first-class cabin. By Christ, I needed a little relaxation and luxury when I'd got to the end of one of those jaunts. Sometimes I went on the wagon during the return voyage. Three times around A deck before a boiled-egg breakfast. Into bed alone, while the other salesmen were telling their dirty stories and lining up the triples in the Neptune Bar. (Or, if it was the *Roconia*, the Swordfish Bar.) I used to count the days! Christ knows what I would have done that day in the village if I'd known how long it was going to be before I saw Rio again.

I unbuttoned my shirt and, after wiping the chair-back with a piece of newspaper, hung my clean white shirt upon it. Clean white shirts were the main armament of a European salesman in those days. A frayed collar or a gravy stain would place you among the poor whites or half-caste locals trying to get a pass, or a visa, or a passage, or a dowry or Christ-knows-what they were all trying to get. Every waiting-room was packed with dozens of them, camping there with wives and screaming kids. Once you sat down among them, you'd never get in to sell anyone anything.

The girl watched me take off my shirt and she pulled open the bodice of her petticoat and blew down there. She looked up to see me watching her and smiled. 'It's hot, no?'

'It's hot, *sí*,' I said. She even spoke like something out of a bad film. 'So open the bloody window more, you stupid bitch.'

She didn't show any anger. She never did. They are like that, these girls; they've all got a trace of Indian in them. Calm, see, and patient. Some night, I told myself, she'll cut your sodding throat and there won't be a whisper of noise.

'It will only open as far as that, Alberto. There is a bar fixed to the balcony.'

'Like buggery there is,' I said, 'artful bleeders!' She was right. There was metal bar bolted to the balcony so that the window would open enough to ventilate the room but not enough for anyone to step out on to the balcony. At least, not wide enough for me to step out on to the balcony. The girl might squeeze through. Still, she'd never be able to climb down the pipe, and the drop was thirty feet or more. She'd probably break her back, legs or something. You know what birds are like.

I was cooler by the window. She went and sat down on the fleabitten old bed. I heard the brass frame of it creak but I didn't look around. A bus came down the main street. How it failed to hit someone I'll never know. There were chickens and cats and dogs and Indians and kids screaming their stupid heads off and running out to meet it. The driver didn't care, but by some strange

152

alchemy when the dust settled around the halted bus there were no casualties except in the sense that they were all casualties.

'What do you mean?' she said.

'I mean they are all casualties,' I repeated. 'Poor bastards. You should come over here and see them trying to get into that bus. There must be fifty on the roof and they are chucking boxes and things down to make room for more.'

'Will they get to the coast?'

'They'll get to the coast all right,' I said grimly, 'if they walk there stark naked.' I turned to her, I wanted to explain that she'd be no better off down there with them. 'They'll get a mile down the road and there'll be a roadblock. The soldiers will strip them and turn the bus over to this bugger Manio. It's obvious, isn't it? That's just what he needs for moving his half-baked army from this road to the capital and then back again if needed.'

'His army is not much good?' she said. She was a sarcastic cow, always having a go at me in that quiet way, pretending to be so bloody complaisant. She knew it was my policy never to criticize the police or the army or even the rebels of any country to which I regularly travelled. It's a good rule, because first you may only think things, next you have a couple of drinks and you start saying them. There was a fellow named Murdoch – best bloody rep we ever had – remember old Norman Murdoch? No one could ever teach him to stay off the subject of the dago authorities. He did three years in some poxy prison up-country, and would have done eight, but there was a revolution and he got out along with the shoot-up artists. By that time he could speak one of the hill dialects like a native, and his Spanish was so vernacular I could hardly understand a word he said. He could have made his fortune after that but he wouldn't come back no more. He lost his nerve, I suppose. He ended up an assistant poxy personnel manager in Birmingham.

'His army is *valiente*, *muy valiente*,' I said.

'Why does the driver go?' she said. I was looking at the bus again, the driver was a regular bloody Ramon Novarro: shiny, long black hair, flashing white teeth. Perhaps it's all that bloody maize muck they eat. I touched the bald patch on my head and searched out my fillings with the tip of my tongue.

'Who know?' I answered. 'Perhaps he's one of General Manio's people. Perhaps he's got a wife who nags the arse off him. Perhaps he just doesn't give a shit.' I picked at the Victorian wallpaper and tore a strip of it away from the wall. Then I looked at the picture over the wash basin: Napoleon taking a sword from some bugger. That's the way the generals fought their wars, like bloody horse-racing. All they lost was their sodding swords. They were never locked up in lousy, nitty hotels in some little stench-pit of a jungle bus-stop, waiting for some punch-drunk wogs to put them up against the wall.

'You shouldn't lose your temper,' she said. 'It makes you smoke too much.'

'It's all bloody fine and nice for you,' I said. 'Any time you feel like it, you can clear off. I've seen that bloody sentry eyeing you every time he comes in with the food. You can choose,' I said, 'between death and a fate worse than it.' I laughed. It seemed quite a good joke, considering I wasn't sitting back in the Savage Club with a glass in my hand. But she didn't laugh; she howled.

You can't ever tell about women. I didn't want that poxy great sentry in there again. Twice during the night he'd come in without knocking, hoping to catch us at it, I suppose, the randy sod. So I lent her a handkerchief and told her to blow her nose and how much I loved her and all that crap. I'm telling it like this now, but I must admit I was a bit gone on her at that time. I mean, she needn't

154

have stayed on with me after the rebel *policías* took me off the bus. They didn't even know she was travelling with me then, but she got my case down and arranged for the driver to . . .

'Here, what did you do with my sample case?' I said. 'The black shiny case that I always keep with me.'

'It's at the bus garage,' she said. 'With your valise.'

'Oh, yes, bloody marvellous,' I said. 'And you think that will have lasted five minutes with this fleabitten gang of comic-opera desperadoes.'

'Be calm, Alberto,' she said. She always called me Alberto. 'They will not steal your baggage,' she fiddled around in her handbag. 'I have the receipt.'

'When will you be able to get it into that stupid little head of yours that there is a war going on around here.'

'A *revolución*,' she said.

'Oh! I stand corrected: *a revolución*.' But my sarcasm was lost on her.

The lino was cracked and rotten, like damp cardboard. When I kicked up a corner of it with my toe, a battalion of ants came out in review formation. They weren't the dangerous little brown sods but I kicked the lino back in place before I saw any of those too. Under the bed there was a chamber pot decorated with a design of English roses, and there was a matching jug and bowl on the washstand. When the sun crept up as far as the marble top you could see the criss-cross lines of spider's-web that anchored it to the scalloped woodwork and tiles of the splashback. I opened the drawer of the wash-stand. It had been carefully lined with pages from a Spanish-language newspaper. The paper had gone brown and the print had faded so as to make it almost undecipherable. There was some little bugger named Salvador something standing up and getting himself married surrounded by a lot of grinning relations. By now, I thought, he's had fifteen kids and is getting a pension from the cement factory. Also in the drawer there was a hairpin and a dozen dead flies. I slammed it closed.

'How about you talking that young sentry into getting my case of samples?' I said. 'Say it's your spare knickers or something.'

'Is this what you care about, your samples?'

'Listen, duchess,' I said. 'Without my samples, no orders. No orders, no moolah. Get my drift, do you?'

'I'll try,' she said.

'You get it, Delilah,' I replied. 'Or you've lost your meal ticket to Rio.'

She shrugged, but I knew she would do her best. She knew which side her bread was buttered. A war, pardon me, a *revolución*, blowing up in my face was going to be a big laugh for Dorkins and Stevens in accounts. They were always making jokes about the money I spent on clients. That was because, in those countries that were my special territory, there prevailed an ancient and honourable tradition of *manos puercas*: dirty hands, although grasping bloody hands would be my description. Packet, Drew and Drew (Birmingham) Ltd, my employers, preferred that these payments should be entered under 'entertaining' on my sheets. So sometimes they did look very top heavy. But by now I was used to their stale jokes. Neither of them had travelled farther than Yarmouth for their holidays and even then they wore handkerchiefs knotted at each corner on their heads, to prevent sunstroke. Once when Stevens went to London to do some costings you'd have thought he was packing to go on an expedition to Nepal. And how much should I tip the doorman, and how much to the page, and how much to the wine waiter. 'You're going to live a rich life, aren't you, Stevens?' I said. 'Where are you going to get your bed and flipping brekkers, Buckingham Palace?' Dorkins saw the joke but Stevens took a month to get over it.

Both of the bastards would laugh now, though. They envied me my two trips a year. They should have come along some time. They would have looked with renewed affection upon their little semis on the Wolverhampton Road.

I kicked the skirting-board and had the satisfaction of hearing a few pounds of desiccated plaster avalanche down under the paper. I kicked the bulge and a white cloud puffed from the split. I heard the key turn in the door so I moved away from the torn wallpaper and stood near the wash-stand. The Sergeant came in. A big fat peasant with one finger missing and a festering boil on his neck. No wonder he was in a bad temper. I made a special effort not to irritate the cow's son but already my resolve was beginning to wear thin.

I said, '*Muy estimado sargento . . .*'

He waved me quiet with his damaged hand. With the other he unclipped the flap of his holster. I recognized the butt of the pistol. It was a 9-mm Mauser; goodness only knows how many of them the Germans must have made during the war. There were enough of them in South America to fight World War One all over again. 'Lieutenant Costa,' announced the Sergeant, like a flunkey at some bloody city gutbash.

The Lieutenant was quite another thing: a lawyer or accountant I would have guessed. *Despicar* merchants they call them in this part of the world. You can see one like him sitting outside the cafés of any little seaport of South America. They sit around and argue and drink the lousy local brandy until they go hoarse. And they hope that some poor little bugger of a first mate will screw up the bills of lading, or not notice a couple of crates being lifted on the sly, and suddenly there will be ructions; abuse, police and customs will descend and start nailing up official-looking pieces of paper to the mast. The only solution is to pay some local mouthpiece, like this

157

Lieutenant, a wad of paper money to sort it all out. It's not so easy to pull with a skipper, of course, but if it's only the chief they'll have him thinking they are going to impound his boat and have him in the Hague International Court if he doesn't hand them a month's pay. I'd always watched out for *despicar* bandits when I travelled and I had this little officer down as one from the moment I first saw him.

'Albert Sampson?' said the officer. It's in my passport, so there wasn't much point in denying it. This Lieutenant Costa walked around behind me and pretended to peer out of the window but I knew that he was just getting an eyeful of the girl. She was still on the bed and not taking any notice of him. 'You work for Packet, Drew and Drew?'

'That's it,' I said.

The girl said, 'Lieutenant, if you are going to talk business with my husband, may I go to the bus garage and collect one of the other cases?'

'I will send one of my men,' said the Lieutenant. That's bloody torn it, I thought. But the girl was up to that one. 'There are clothes of mine . . . I need to sort through the cases and find clean things.'

He looked back to me. He knew she wasn't my wife, not with Spanish of the sort that she spoke. Stranger things have happened, but he was no fool. He looked at her for a long time before he nodded. She went behind the broken folding-screen to put her black frock on. She'd worn a pink one on the bus, but in a little town like this only one sort of woman wore any shade of red. The lieutenant nodded his approval when he saw that she was wearing a more suitable colour.

He waited for the sound of her footsteps to go down the stairs before he spoke again. 'Which way did you come?'

158

'You know which way I came,' I said. 'From Innocenti. Your men took me off the bus to Port Sargossa.'

'And from there?'

I pulled a face. 'A ship, I suppose. Anything going down the coast would be cleaner and more comfortable than the bus. To tell you the truth, I can't stand the heat and humidity at this time of the year.'

'It will get much worse.'

'I know that,' I said. 'I've been coming here since 1922. Never missed a year. It gets hotter, wetter and more stinking every bloody year.'

'Or do you get cooler, Mr Sampson?'

'That's a good one,' I said, and laughed as much as I could.

I looked at his uniform. It fitted him well. He even had linen cuffs that made a white starched interval between the dark-green sleeves and his pale hands, and more clean linen between his rank badges and his well-scrubbed neck. This uniform had definitely been made for Costa, so he must have been one of the regular officers that had joined Manio's forces up here in the north. One and a half battalions, the rumours said, were disloyal to the government. As a gesture, the Lieutenant was wearing one of the green-and-red armbands that the revolutionaries said represented crops and fire. If things went wrong it would be easy to remove it, and then he would be a government man again.

He was looking out of the window. There was no movement on the street now except a couple of dogs lashing the flies away with angry tails, and a drunken Indian flat on his face outside the Flour Distribution Agency that had been empty for four years. At one time it had always been slightly whiter than the other buildings but this year's rain had changed even that.

'You are letting the buses continue?' I said.

'My orders are to remain here. I remain here. I do nothing. More orders will come.'

There was an electric fan fixed to the ceiling, a merry-go-round for bored mosquitoes. It revolved so slowly that it scarcely disturbed the stale hot-wet air but it made a continuous screech as it turned. 'You took me off the bus,' I challenged.

'That was the only order,' he agreed.

'You came here specially to take me off that bus?'

'I cannot say. There may be other reasons. Other orders may come.'

I went close to the window. By pushing my face against the glass I could see almost as far as the bus station where they had come aboard for us and made the other passengers stand around for two hours while they questioned them. I couldn't see the girl.

'She's all right,' said the officer. I nodded and tried to look concerned in the way that an anxious European husband should be for a beautiful young wife with a figure that shows too clearly through her thin cotton dress. It was so hot that drips of sweat ran down the side of my nose. Even the Lieutenant dabbed at his forehead with a handkerchief.

'And your case,' said Costa, 'that will be all right too. It's heavy, of course, but my men will help her carry it here.'

'*Muchísimas gracias*,' I said. The cunning little sod. I knew I would have to be very careful of him.

He said, 'The war has caught you by surprise, eh?' I nodded.

A war! Was it any wonder that I was going around thumping the furniture and kicking the bedstead. I'd been travelling through South America for years and I had the reputation for being able to smell a war when it was only a drunken whisper. I'd underestimated this Manio, though. 'Manio the peasant' they used to call him. An

good as Webley for use in field conditions: by which I mean mud. I was also carrying a 9-mm lever-action carbine and a shoddy, but dirt cheap, two-inch mortar. Add nearly a gross of PDD fuses and you'll understand why the Sergeant was out of breath.

'It's the new fuse that I'm interested in,' said Lieutenant Costa.

'I should think so,' I said, 'it's ten years ahead of anything on the market.' I gave him the entire sales talk. I'd worked it out so that as I demonstrated I had a chance to repeat each of the sales points several times. He dismissed the adapters, which were various bits of metal that clamped the fuse to half a dozen Mills grenades or to slabs of gun cotton, because, as he said, you could do that with a piece of cord or wire. But old Drew had been quite right to include those adapters because any number of superannuated idiots in the Ministries and the purchasing departments thought they were very ingenious. In any case, they helped to fix it in people's minds that these fuses could be set to fire any size of explosion for almost any type of job from a bridge to a bicycle. I used to say that: 'From a bridge to a bicycle,' I told them. But that stuff cut no ice with this Lieutenant Costa. All he wanted was a demonstration of the Dialawate: a tension spring that could be changed so that the detonator would operate only when the selected weight – or more – was upon it. The advantage was that a soldier on foot didn't set off an anti-tank charge. I mean, that would be an awfully expensive way to kill one infantryman.

When the girl came back she stood by the door and listened to my sales talk. Her eyes were stuck to my hands as I turned the dial and made enough before but the various settings. She'd heard it the time. Or so I she still managed probably though

163

That night long after Costa had gone, and a long time after we finished the mess of *frijoles*, *tortillas* and thimble-sized cups of coffee that tasted like iron filings she spoke of the fuses.

'The *teniente* wants you to go to Sagorino tomorrow?'

'He can want on,' I said. 'I just sell this stuff, I don't go fighting wars with it.'

'It's a *revolución*.'

'I don't care if it's a bloody bar mitzvah,' I said. 'I'm not going to get myself shot at.'

'You think your fuse may not work and the *teniente* will be angry?'

'Of course it will work. You've seen me demonstrate them.'

'Does it matter that this demonstration will be real? You can put the mines in the road long before the *Federalistas* arrive.'

'Look, I've told you, no. Get me? No. No. No. No. Now shut your mouth and go to sleep.'

But she had planted an idea. I knew that Gatling had often demonstrated his gun during battles of the American Civil War, and I knew that the Dutchman Fokker had flown on a patrol with his synchronized machine-guns. And those two punters had done very nicely, thank you, as my memory served me.

By the same time the following night I had every reason to regret my decision. Ever see the jungle at dawn? White steam comes belching out of the trees like old cabbage on the boil. And the stink is like old cabbage-water, too. After eight long hours of climbing in and out of the bush arguing with Costa about the best place to
to my minefield, that stink of sour putrefaction clung
The girl look that no amount of washing could ever
dusk, I stagger
amazement when, almost at
a stiff drink. Seeing

myself in the mirror helped me understand why. The khaki shirt was dark with sweat, and my cotton trousers were torn in two places and marked on knees and buttocks with patches of the mustard-coloured earth that you get in the north of the province. One of Costa's men had twisted his ankle and slid fifty yards down a gully, and all of us were pretty well whacked. To make it worse, I couldn't make Costa understand the basic principles of minelaying. He was still at the boy-scout stage of thinking that it was a way to destroy transport or personnel.

'Look, Costa. If you want to blow up the bloody *Federalistas* and their armoured cars you'd do better with your gun cotton and a dynamo exploder Mark V. Mines are just a way of *delaying* an enemy. Delay, you understand? You worry them: they have to bring up sappers and bugger about prodding the whole sector. Or you can force them to use the road you want them on. Delay, see? The casualties you inflict are just a bonus.'

But it was no use. He insisted that we put them down on the approach to the village of Juon. His reasoning being that he could have a couple of machine-guns hidden in the loft of the grain store and spray the wreckage while they were running around in panic. Also, he said, they might come along that wide stretch of road two cars abreast. Ha bloody ha.

I could see the San Carlo mountains from this window. Dark blue icebergs with mauve tops where the sun disappeared behind them. It was frightening to think that that stinking jungle stretched hundred of miles, all the way to the Pacific. Full of screaming, catcalling birds and animals, spiders as big as a human hand and snakes every colour of the rainbow sliding through the dark, dripping vegetation. Ugh. It was bad enough in the daytime, but as the light went the prospect of it was my special nightmare.

The girl had run a very hot bath for me. She took away

165

my filthy clothes and gave them to the old woman who cleaned the room. They'd need boiling to be rid of half the smell. She'd bought some lemon essence in the village; raw alcohol with oils added to it. She rubbed some on me after my bath. It was funny how she seemed to know what I'd need in advance. If this morning she'd mentioned the idea of an alcohol rub I would have told her she was crazy. I suppose she sort of loved me in her way. I didn't go along with that stuff, it could only lead to a life in some rotten little house and a job as a clerk, but I could see the advantages sometimes.

'You were right about Costa,' I admitted. 'You said he'd keep his word. I think he will.'

'He has a job to do.'

'Then I bloody wish he'd show a bit more common. His idea of a minefield would make you weep. What he can't bloody get into his thick swede is: mines go right where they are expected to go. He keeps trying to think of surprises.'

'Then you should insist,' said the girl.

'It's all right for you. I'm his *peón* until he's finished with this fart-arsing little *fiesta*.'

'You are *flamenco*, Alberto, and that foreignness blinds you to the fact that he needs you. He wants your advice.'

'That's very funny, seeing as how we've put the mines down in what are just about the two worst places on the road. All the *Federalistas* need do is chop down a couple of trees, prod the verge and drive the other armoured cars around the edge of the wreckage. Tomorrow we are going to do the tunnel. The tunnel!'

'How would you do it, Alberto?'

'How would I do it? I tell you how I would do it. I'd forget about mining the tunnel road for a start. He could block the road near the tobacco plantation just as well. Nothing could get off that road and cross that bloody swamp, and he'd have the armoured cars for his own use

166

instead of in a tunnel under a bloody mountain of rock. Anyway, his wholesale bloody attitude with the explosives – ten slabs of gun cotton at a time – will make those armoured cars look like a handful of small change! It's his bloody war, I know, but those cars cost a few pennies. Anyway, I know who will be laughing next week.'

'You will?'

'Too bloody Irish, I will! You'll hear the greatest commotion since Mum caught her tits in the mangle!'

'Can you be so *loco*, Alberto, that you don't know it is better that this fighting ends with the *teniente* feeling grateful?'

See what I mean about cunning? But she was right. And I was quick to see it.

'You must shout, Alberto. Men like the *teniente* are not truly of the *revolución*. They joined the army of General Manio because they need a *caudillo*. You must command him.'

What's that old saying that the upper classes despise the workers, while the middle classes are scared stiff of them? Well she had the middle-class *teniente* taped all right. 'You're a dark horse,' I told her.

'You say things that I do not understand, Señor Sampson.'

'Come here, Delilah. You don't need that nightdress for a moment.'

The next day I drove out to Juon with Costa and four of his half-witted soldiers and I started digging the mines out again, using a bayonet and a pair of pliers. There were ten mines across the road set in a trellis pattern. When we first got there I made a special point of walking down the line of them. Costa pulled me aside anxiously, for I'd pretended to blunder upon them. But I knew that the fuse was set so that nothing less than a one-ton weight could trigger it. Costa smiled his relief and I nudged him in the ribs.

'I would have been sorry, Señor Sampson, truly sorry.'

'I can imagine,' I said. 'We haven't started repositioning them yet.'

Costa was quite hurt. 'But I mean it,' he protested. 'I was hoping that we could work together until the revolution is complete.'

'Now look, Costa, don't get any ideas. Our deal is that I'll fix this armoured column for you. But after your little *corrida* we are quits: you pay for the fuses and we scarper.'

'We are not thieves. We will pay you, not only for the fuses but also for your time. I have spoken with General Manio about you. I have suggested that we pay you one thousand dollars.'

'American?'

'It would probably be the most convenient for your travels.'

'You have so much money available?'

'Señor Sampson, the *Federalistas* have eight Daimler armoured cars and five hundred peasant conscripts. Most of the regular soldiers have already come over to Manio. When we have disposed of this column of cars there will be nothing to stop us driving into the capital and writing cheques on any bank there.'

'Would I get a thousand every week?' I said already slicing the wiring off the fuses, using a breadknife to dig under the fuse into the soft dusty road.

'Certainly,' said Costa.

By the time I got the last of the fuses I was being careful to make it seem very difficult. I told Costa and his boys to take cover as I lifted each charge, and instead of cutting them immediately I pulled a few faces and put on a worried frown.

When we'd lifted all the mines I asked him what he proposed. He had some fantastic plan for bottling them up in the tunnel. I laughed. 'You're a regular bleeding *fenómeno*, you are.' That's what the newspapers call bright young kids who think they are going to be famous bullfighters.

The *teniente* said, 'Then tell me what you would do.'

Once he let me have my say, I gave it to him: right out of the *Manual, Field Works (all Arms), Sappers, for the use of*. I told him that mines were no bloody use for attacking a column of armoured cars, unless perhaps you stood by the roadside and chucked them at the enemy. Oh, yes, he says nodding his head, like I'd just given him an idea for the ultimate deterrent. I told him that even for defence you need a thousand of the buggers before you can call it a minefield. Anyway, seeing the disappointed look in his eyeballs, we put a couple of dozen PDD specials in a triple box each side of the crossroads and wired up some little odds and sods of Ammonal that had probably earned long-service medals. It looked a bit damp so I didn't handle it myself, but luckily there were no accidents with it.

One of Costa's lads gave us the alarm signal on a five-inch heliograph. Yes, a heliograph – takes you back a bit, eh? I'll tell you that when I saw it flashing on the hillside I felt like an extra in *The Four Feathers*. There wasn't much time to think after that because the *Federalistas* were coming down the road. There were three infantry companies. Straggling like buggery and armed with those antique Martini-Henrys that that little fellow Kennedy was doing at five dollars a time.

Humberto – that was Costa's first name – was in a derelict mission building, with his Maxims firing across what had once been a tobacco plantation. I stayed in the ditch, crouching low enough to avoid any stray shots that those trigger-happy clowns behind me might send my way.

There was a pause in the firing at his Maxims changed ammo boxes. So I stood up and signalled Humberto to bring his boys forward in open order. They thought I was crazy at first, then they thought I was a military genius. Me! Yes, it makes me laugh, too. Of course, I knew those Martini-Henrys. Kennedy had sold that consignment three times. He traded back when the customer found that the extractors worked about one time in ten. I laughed. Now it was this customer's turn to discover that flaw in the merchandise. *Caveat* bloody *emptor*, Perce, as I said to Humberto. Kennedy would no doubt be around soon to offer the Federalistas a trade-in for them.

I heard the armoured cars coming past the crossroads long before I saw them. They were a long way behind the infantry, and the high ground between prevented them hearing the noise of the Maxims. The sound of the engines made a fiendish din as it echoed against the narrow rock cutting, and some of the soldiers gave yells and whoops to hear their voices echo. They were like a lot of kids playing cowboys. Poor sods, I felt sorry for them.

When the first car came out into the light I could see it was real Lawrence-of-Arabia stuff. They weren't Daimlers, they were those armoured Austins. Four-and-three-quarter-ton jobs, with 50-horse engines. The Russians bought some in 1915 and there had been quite a few knocking about cheap since the Armistice. These had been converted back to solid tyres. Economical, but they must have given a rough ride over those roads. Imagine that 108-mm armour closed down under a tropical sun, Christ!

The twin turrets were like two dustbins, remember? They had a good traverse and excellent depression, as I remembered it. Not that I need have worried, the gunners were having a siesta or were drunk. Both, probably! I could have walked out and stolen their hub-caps for all the gunners did about it for the first five minutes. Some of the infantry officers and a few cripples were sitting on

170

the cars. That didn't help them much. I put my head down and triggered the first charge. The Austin in front went down on one knee like a rhino taking a double .470 between the eyes and snorting its bad breath over you. The radiator disappeared into a cloud of steam and the wheel went past me up the road, and so did pieces of the poor bugger sitting on the wing. As I said to Humberto afterwards, I was nearly hit in the earhole by half a dozen loin chops and a gristly 8-oz rump steak. Humberto had a good laugh at that one, he's got a wonderful sense of humour.

That armoured Austin was fair and square in the middle of the road. Nothing could get past it. I pressed the plunger for the charges on the rock face. It was an impressive show. I didn't think we'd bring down the sixty-foot tree. That minor miscalculation meant I had to press my face into the crappy ditch bottom. No matter, there was a neat pile of stones blocking the road behind them, just as I'd promised young Humberto.

The crews of the cars knew they were goners whatever they did. Finally they came out and Humberto shot them with his Maxims, which by now were boiling up alarmingly. That was always the trouble with those water-cooled guns, you could spot them for miles.

Did we have a party that night! I was so blotto that I drove Costa's old Ford into the pond and it was only the quick action of Pedro, the fat sergeant, that saved me from being drowned. He's a nice fellow! In the morning we were all feeling very sorry for ourselves when a motor-cycle messenger came into town to tell us that General Manio had been killed. Humberto was beside himself, he must have liked that fellow Manio. Sobbing and shouting, he was. He was full of ideas for a military burial in Manio's home village: soldiers firing rifles in the air. All that army crap, you know. I scotched that. I recruited

171

every peasant we could get to clear the road for those armoured cars.

Then we brought Manio's body from the coast and made up a sort of armoured funeral procession and trooped it into the capital. Manio ponged something rotten by then, I can tell you. We were having temperatures of ninety-plus. But we draped the coffin with flowers and leaves. It was a simple boxwood job that I chose, just like the peasants use. I turfed him out of the mahogany one: too bloody posh by half! The soldiers wore flowers and leaves, too. Red flowers and green leaves, the colours of their *revolución*, you see.

Talk about a success. Every village we went through gave us another fifty peasants walking behind us, crying like they were going to burst. In the capital it was even more dramatic. The main plaza – that I renamed Plaza Manio – was packed with people. Luckily I'd had the foresight to arrange for a microphone and amplifier so that we could be heard as far as what is now Sampson Boulevard. I kept Costa near to the amplifier controls because we'd both read *Julius Caesar*, if you know what I mean.

I remember it all so clearly, and yet other memories have grown dim. It's a long time ago, of course. I was sorry the girl died that same year. It was a miserable Christmas for me, without her. The doctor said she'd had fever for quite a time, and I suppose the fact that Costa and I went woman-mad during the first few months of power didn't help much. But I gave her a solid marble tomb and a service conducted by the Bishop, so I made it up to her in a way. That religious stuff was important to her. I suppose she had me earmarked for conversion.

Of course, a lot has happened to you since those days of which I write. World War Two and so on. I remember how angry you were when I made it a capital offence to sell arms in the province. Many of the other companies

172

didn't believe that I meant it, but we shot a Belgian fellow from Brownings and an American travelling in sporting rifles and we didn't have any more trouble after that. And never a whisper of *revolución*, either. I got going with tarmac roads from here to each province so that they couldn't be mined like the dirt roads. This plus lorried infantry was my first priority.

Salesmen are escorted here from the border and I see them in person. I know the score: I give them their commission in full before the deal is settled and *then* we talk about the price. Set a thief to catch a thief, Humberto always says. He's my Minister of Security and he loves it. He's got White half-tracks now; next year I'm hoping to give him Schmeissers to replace his Garands.

It's funny to think that the new Mr Drew wasn't even born when all this happened. I'm sure I'd never recognize the Packet, Drew and Drew factory now. Certainly it was Stevens's insistence on tendering for the proximity fuse in 1943 that was the turning-point. I've followed the progress of the firm, I see your adverts in the *Defense Review* and I felt proud when I heard that PDD (Guidance Systems) Inc, New Jersey, helped to put the first man on the moon. In a way, you see, I've always felt that it was PD and D who put me here.

Yours sincerely,
GENERAL ALBERTO SAMPSON
(*Commander of Freedom*)
Palacio de Libertad
Innocenti

Action

John Dover knew how his story must begin. Not in the imposing old mansion that was used as an Officers' Mess. That was full of leather armchairs, Irish linen and passable food. It was like a London club, except that the voices from the anteroom were too shrill and guest nights too much of a rumpus. The Mess was a warm comfortable place. That came later, much later.

John Dover's story began in a place that was cold, wet and miserable: a place where men would go only to sleep. Or try to sleep. B Flight pits was such a place. 'Pit' was slang for bed, and there were forty beds in tiny hardboard cubicles in the four tar-black corrugated-iron huts on the exposed side of the RAF airfield at Grebe. They were far beyond B Flight. Even beyond the Repair Party hangar, where crippled bombers were parked waiting to be dissected and disembowelled by factory-trained civvies who made more money each week than the commanding officer.

Originally the pits were a shelter for ground crews who spent their duty hours out there on the edge of the world where the wind honed its edge on the wet fenland of East Anglia. It was only after a Canadian squadron had arrived the previous autumn – bringing an unusually high proportion of officer aircrews – that the pits became the OFFICERS' MESS ANNEXE. OUT OF BOUNDS TO OTHER RANKS EXCEPT ON DUTY. The notice had long since been mud-spattered, knocked askew and broken. Finally it disappeared into one of the temperamental iron stoves that kept a haze of dirty smoke hanging over the place.

In winter there was nowhere colder than the pits.

Anything that might help to warm the huts was tried. Parachute elastic was fixed to the doors to spring them closed; stolen coal was piled under the beds, and every window was sealed with yards of insulating tape. Devoid of ventilation, the huts smelled of unwashed bodies and ancient blankets. There was no running water, and the duty crews had grown tired of refilling the fire buckets that hung in the corridors. They were now cobwebbed and dusty.

Pilot Officer John Dover was the man in Room 33. It was the third room on the right if you entered Hut 4 from the village side. Not that you could get in from the other end – the draughty end – because that was permanently locked to prevent the hut being used as a short-cut in rainy weather. Dover couldn't remember any other sort of weather. The rain dripping from his overcoat had made a large white mark on the lino inside the door. However, compared with some of the rooms, Dover's was luxurious. There was a crudely fashioned reading-light rigged over the iron bedstead, a shelf full of battered paperbacks and a torn armchair – rescued from the dump – with its stuffing supplemented with a buckshee overcoat.

On the wall there was a snapshot of Dover's Lancaster bomber – 'Santa Claus' – with Dover standing under the nose. He wouldn't allow the whole crew to be photographed together because so many of the old-timers vowed that Fortune took a fast revenge upon crews that did so.

Under the photo there was a sectional drawing of an Avro Lancaster clipped from *The Aeroplane* magazine. It was almost indecent in its revelation of each nut and bolt, each spar and former of the great machine that Dover had flown to within ten thousand feet of so many German cities. There was a calendar above the drawing. Red pencil marks dated each trip: twenty-three red marks, seven to go.

Dover wished that there were no more to go. Not even the most genial of his instructors had seen Dover as a natural pilot. In fact he suspected that he passed the flying course only because he'd never once complained about the air-sickness that dogged him right through it. Even now, after 250 hours in Lancs, he still suffered nausea when the weather was bad. On his twentieth trip – to Essen – the weather had closed in to ten-tenths cloud. He'd circled the whole of Yorkshire trying to find an aerodrome clear enough to land upon. The strain of this, following the stress he'd suffered over the heavily defended target, had caused him to vomit for almost and hour. Luckily his engineer had been close enough to take the controls. Dover himself had taken over for the actual landing, but after that he'd been almost carried from the aircraft. The blokes were wonderful: not one of them mentioned the fact at any time. But now Dover knew that air-sickness could be totally incapacitating. Sometimes he worried what would happen to his crew if he suffered it again.

John Dover inhaled deeply of the cold air. In winter dusk came early, just as it had nearly thirty years ago when he lived on this field, in this dilapidated hut that became a pigsty. He could hear a Lanc on the circuit. The trees of Dirty Lane hid the great machines as they passed over Grebe Fen village. When they came into sight to the right of the church steeple you could watch out for the bank of the wings as they came on to finals. You could tell then: you could tell if they were badly shot up or the driver was not at his best. 'Not at his best' was the Wingco's way of saying half dead. That Wingco: a cold fish. The red Very lights had already been fired to keep the other planes circling and clear of the cripple. The sky behind the church was dark, and he couldn't see the aeroplane. He felt for his spectacles and put them on before he realized that the sound he could hear was

176

traffic on the Great North Road. The planes had all landed a quarter of a century ago; there were no more to come. The blackboards had long since been wiped clean, the telegrams sent, the widows paid, the war won.

'Have you seen enough, John?'

'I thought it was . . .'

'Yes.'

'The sky was like this. But it wasn't quite as cold.'

'You were younger then, John. You feel the cold more now.'

'Remember?'

'Yes, I remember.'

The young pilot watched the electric kettle boil as he measured two spoonfuls of tea into a battered metal pot.

'It's dangerous to plug a kettle into the light,' said Childs. He was younger than Dover. A fresh-faced youngster with medical officer's badges on his lapels.

Dover poured the hot water carefully. He had no wish to scald himself. 'More dangerous,' he inquired affably, 'than flying to Essen?'

'Why find out?' said Childs. He put milk into both cups.

'It's only bad weather that frightens me,' admitted Dover. 'And that's when I get sick.'

'It's evasive action that makes most chaps queasy,' said Childs. 'Everyone has a weak spot: I knew one fellow who'd done two tours. He said he always felt sick over the target. OK all the way there, OK all the way back, just over the target.'

'Is that neurotic?'

'Of course it is, we're all neurotic. The way I see it, Ben, if you weren't neurotic you wouldn't be alert enough to do the job you do.' They call him Ben as a joke.

'Is that what your old man says, Childsy?' Childs's father was a doctor too. His opinion was often quoted.

177

Childs nodded. He watched Dover going through all the pockets of his best blue uniform. 'What is it, John?'

'The doll.'

'When did you see it last?'

'This morning. I had it this morning.' Dover tipped three dirty blue shirts, some collars and a torn vest out of a box that came from under his bed. He raked through the soiled clothing with his fingers. He squeezed each pocket to be sure that no celluloid doll was hiding in them. 'No one could have taken it,' murmured John Dover, 'surely?'

'For Christ's sake, Ben!'

'The trouble is, if it dropped into the mud it would be trodden in and no one would see it now that it's dark.'

'It will turn up in the morning.'

'Perhaps we'll . . .' Dover didn't finish what he was about to say. He rubbed his face and loosened the sheepskin flying-jacket. His face was flushed and shiny. Perhaps he'd not return in the morning; Childs knew what he'd been about to say.

The old man shivered as he remembered his fears. Some of the words he heard, others were merely inside his head. He moved nearer to the windows of the hut in order to peer inside. He could see the two airmen and wanted to shout advice to them. One learned a lot in twenty-five years, or was it nearer thirty years? A man learns a different set of values.

'If you think your lucky doll is that important, you shouldn't fly,' said Childs.

'That would look great on my medical file, wouldn't it?'

'Just unfit to fly. I don't have to give a reason. That's why they have reserve crews, isn't it?'

'Keep looking, Doc. It's here somewhere.'

'It's five to,' said Childs.

'Will you keep looking? It's a little pink doll with a

178

green-paper skirt. Parsons – my Rear Gunner – won it at a shooting gallery in Blackpool.'

'You told me.'

'Seemed like a good omen; him being the Rear Gunner and all.'

'The crew bus will be leaving.'

'You'll keep looking, Stan?' It was the first time that Dover had used his friend's first name. Until now it had been Childsy or Doc, but never his real name.

'I'll start at the door and go through everything again.'

'We won't take off for another hour.' Dover put his peaked cap on and glanced in the mirror. Then he shuffled through the postcards and official forms that were tucked behind the mirror frame, but no doll was there.

'Ben,' said Childs, pushing the door closed again, 'on my last unit some of the pilots tested their magnetos too many times before take-off.'

'Did they,' said Dover impassively.

'The motors overheated. They had to scrub in case of a mechanical fault.'

Dover didn't answer.

Childs continued, 'They couldn't be blamed for making sure about the mags.'

'How did you hear about it?'

'The Engineering Officer noticed it. He mentioned it to me so that . . .' His voice trailed away.

'And you want me to try it?' Dover flushed at the thought of having his name mentioned to the MO as a possible 'lack of confidence'. The fact that the MO was his friend made the prospect not better but far worse.

'Once. It can happen to anyone once: just nerves, a natural thing.'

'OK, Childsy,' said Dover. Childs wasn't quite sure whether Dover meant he had understood him or not. Dover gave a jerky palms-down salute like they had seen in some old Hollywood film. His smile didn't hide the tight lines of anxiety that had appeared on his grey, shrivelled face.

'If I don't – ' said Childs.

'Then forget it. It's not that important.' The outside door slammed as Dover stamped out over the metal grating that was clogged with ancient mud. There was a rattle as his bicycle was moved from the rack alongside the corrugated hut. 'Good luck, Ben,' said Childs softly. It was more prayer than farewell, for Dover was far out of earshot.

One after another Childs heard the Lancasters run-up their engines. Dabs of rain hit the dirty windows, and the reading light, by which Childs continued his search, made a tiny dot of gold inside each raindrop. The storm clouds had sunk lower and lower until the ceiling became dangerously little, but tonight was ordered as 'a maximum effort' and it would not be scrubbed.

Childs wondered how much of his friend's anxiety was due to the lost mascot, how much to the tough target – Essen again – and how much to the bad weather. Predisposition poor, thought Childs.

'Did I call you Childsy, Stanley?'

'Sometimes you did.'

'How frightful,' said Dover.

'We were young.'

'As young as those two?'

'Younger,' said Childs, 'and far more stupid.'

'A man shouldn't be allowed this agony,' said Dover.

'It was your own decision, John.'

Even as the two old men watched, the night passed and dawn came. Easy now to say that it was magical, but his life had passed just as quickly. He looked across to the control tower. It was newly painted, and as pristine as it had been that day in 1943 when he'd first arrived here as a sprog officer with the wings still bright on his tunic.

Childs went back to the pits at midday. It had been a bad one: Santa Claus hadn't returned, nor had O Orange. The Admin Officer was acting as 'effects bod' that week. There was a young airman with him who bundled up Dover's uniforms and dirty linen as the Admin Officer ticked a list. They worked quietly because the pits were full of sleeping officers who had returned from the raid. Now and again there was an anxious cry or some snores, and in the last room someone who could not sleep was stifling his coughs.

'That would be Davidson,' said the old man. 'He's got bronchitis. Never finished his tour, as I remember.'

'No,' said Childs, 'shot down over Hamburg in July '43. During the week of fire raids. One of the first to go, Davidson. On the Monday, I think.'

'Really,' said Dover. It was funny that it had taken him thirty years to find that out. He'd always faintly resented Davidson getting released from his tour so easily.

'And a celluloid doll,' said the airman. He was making three piles: photos and maps for return to the Intelligence Officer, personal effects to be auctioned for the next of kin and a third pile of letters and sometimes photos that were best destroyed. Sometimes the airmen stole the pornographic photos and sold them in the NAAFI.

'Doll,' acknowledged the Admin Officer, adding it to his list. 'Put it with the letters.' He looked up suddenly as Childs came in. 'Hello, Doc, what are you doing here?' He blushed. 'Oh, of course, young Dover. I'm awfully sorry.'

'Where did you find the doll?' said Childs. He picked it up off the dressing-table.

'The doll? Oh, I don't know, just among all his stuff.'

'I didn't go!' shouted the old man. 'The inner port engine was overheating. Ask the engineer, ask any of the

181

fitters, they'll tell you why we didn't go.' His voice had been so loud that everyone stopped to stare at him. They were angry with him, and rightly so. They were doing a job that was difficult enough, without criticism across thirty years from another generation.

'I'm sorry,' said Dover. 'I didn't mean to interrupt.' After all, it was his idea to come, just as Childs had reminded him. They'd all been awfully kind, too, letting him pry and peer into places he had no right to go.

The young man was very understanding. It was not the first time such a thing had happened. Watching one's past unfold before one's eyes must be a terrible strain. Especially when – as now – a man remembered it all so differently.

Dover tried to explain. 'It's just that it wasn't like that.'

'Like what?' said the man.

'That business about the magneto switches. I must explain it to you.'

'Magneto switches?' said the young man. He smiled awkwardly and tried to imagine what the old dotard was talking about. '"Leave it to me, sir, we'll wipe out the U-boat pens if it's the last thing we do,"' he read from a large book. 'They were the only words spoken, sir.'

'I don't remember anything about U-boat pens,' said Dover.

'Don't you worry about it, sir. Even the rushes you saw are nothing like the real thing. Once we get the sound effects and the music on it and get a proper graded print, it will look different again.'

'It was nothing like this,' said Dover sadly. 'Nothing like this at all.'

'You heard that great music?'

'Yes, I heard it,' said Dover.

Childs took the old hero by the arm and spoke quietly to him. 'These film people are leaving out the business about you being afraid, John. And also the mix-up when

182

you tested your magnetos and the Wingco threatened to court-martial you for cowardice. In the film you get shot down over Berlin in the end.'

'But that was in 1945,' said Dover, 'that was my third tour. That was two years later, it was Graz.'

'Yes, yes, yes,' said Childs gently. He was a Harley Street specialist and well used to the petulance of old age. 'But they don't want our war, John. They have writers.'

'It wasn't like that,' protested Air-Marshal Dover, VC, DSC, DFC. The war wasn't like that.'

'It might have been,' said Childs, 'if we'd had their incidental music.'

Twelve Good Men and True

Between the shimmering white peaks of the western Himalayas and the equally white and even more shimmering desert that stretches to the Arabian Sea, there is the Punjab. To cool stations in its lush green foothills, favoured units of the British Army retired each May. After that, life on the plains became so unbearably hot that even the natives sat quite still all day, waiting for the movement of air that sometimes came with dusk. Pooglui was a depot on the hot plains. Sergeant Brand and twelve private soldiers of the Royal Fusiliers were unhappy to go there during the hot season, even for a few hours.

This evening was not cool by the standards of their hill station two hundred miles to the east. The train had taken them through Lahore Junction before the journey south; a circuitous route of over five hundred miles. It had stopped every hour since they boarded it twenty-one hours earlier. They'd eaten their rations soon after departure and although they had bought fruit, nuts, biscuits and sweets during the journey they were now desperate for a glass of beer and some army food.

At Pooglui railway station Sergeant Brand looked for an army official who could provide him with instructions about the next stage of the journey, but after the train departed the station was empty. There were no beggars outside the first-class waiting-room, no vagrants asleep in the toilets and no families tucked up on the platforms. There was not even sweepers to be seen. From somewhere, however – eclipsing the smells of excreta and carbolic – there was the pungent scent of curry. Sergeant Brand followed his nose to find it.

The other twelve soldiers helped each other with their puttees and buttoned up their sweaty tunics. They were yawning and swearing gently to themselves as they buckled together the absurd and mysterious array of webbing pieces with which infantrymen garland themselves.

Sergeant John Douglas Brand was a 'barrack rat'. The son of a Fusilier Sergeant, he'd been born in a military depot, gone to an army school and joined the army as a boy entrant soon after his sixteenth birthday. He'd known no other life but that of a soldier. His face was tanned and prematurely wrinkled by fierce foreign suns. His calloused hands were dextrous and his stride even and purposeful. Without any effort he could project his calm voice across a parade ground and halt a rogue elephant at five hundred paces – or so he claimed when drilling his platoon.

Brand had served in many parts of the world and his speech was littered with bits of Hindi, Arabic, Gurkhali and French. He fought in France from 1914 until 1918. He'd seen his battalion eaten away by casualties, so that the men he'd soldiered with in 1901 now formed an elite group of survivors numbering less than a dozen. It was almost exactly two years since the Armistice, and Brand had spent most of that in India. But India in 1920 wasn't what it was before the war, he reflected. Nor was England; nor was the army; nor was any bloody thing. When he'd been a recruit the sergeants lived like rajahs. Now . . . well, when his number came up in two years' time, he'd not re-enlist. He didn't know what he'd do, but he'd not re-enlist.

Sergeant Brand stopped walking. He opened a door marked STATION MASTER. He'd found the source of the smell. Four wide-eyed railway officials were sitting inside a gloomy office. One of them, lighter skinned than the others, was wearing a hat that showed him to be an

185

official of the Great Indian Peninsular Railway, and to him Brand addressed his question.

'Detachment of Royal Fusiliers for Pooglui guardroom. Know anything about that, Johnny?'

The Indians looked at each other for a moment, then the man with the official cap turned his dark moist eyes to Brand. 'Nothing, sahib.' The other three were bearded in the plaited style of the Sikhs. Brand decided that they were Jats.

'Where's the RTO then, where's the provost?' The smoke from the fire made his eyes water and he opened the door to let the evening air come into the room.

'No one here, Sergeant. Only us. All Indian persons are sent away from Pooglui. After the midnight train we also go.'

'Go?' said Brand. Were they trying to make a fool of him? 'Go where? Where in hell are you going to at midnight?'

'To the next village, sahib. All people go. Army lorries take everyone. At midnight a lorry will come for us.' He lifted the lid of the black iron pot and stirred the contents. There was a smell of ginger, haldi and garlic. Near the cast-iron stove there was a row of freshly made chappatis. They were pale and flecked with meal, like unfired dinner plates awaiting the kiln. Sergeant Brand didn't like native food very much but he would very willingly have sat down to this meal had a detachment of soldiers not been waiting for him – and had he been invited.

'Perhaps you will use the phone, sahib,' suggested the man, and Sergeant Brand cursed his own stupidity for not having thought of it. Brand turned up the wick of the oil lamp so that it made a pool of soft yellow light in the centre of the room. He groped on the cluttered desk to find the telephone and cranked the handle.

'Pooglui Camp guardroom,' he told the operator, '*Jildi, jildi, jildi.*' Through the office window the eastern sky was mauve and the mountains the darkest of purples, like the shiny brinjal fruit. There were no lights anywhere in the village, and he didn't fancy marching men through the dark street of an unlit town. There were stories of restlessness across the whole of India.

Here, not so far from the North-West Frontier, rifles were always chained and locked into the racks at night. Twelve Lee Enfields and his own Webley revolver would make a prize for which plenty of Indians would risk a rope. In the hills one modern rifle could buy a man a house and wives and a lifetime of comfort.

'That's it,' said Brand, 'at the station, *ek dum*.' He listened while, at the other end of the phone, a clerk referred matters to a superior and came back to tell him that a lorry would be there soon. Brand turned to the four Indians who had been watching him with curiosity.

'They're coming,' said Brand. They said nothing. 'See you tomorrow. We'll be on the 10.40 in the morning.'

'Here today, gone tomorrow, sahib,' said the man in the peaked cap and smiled broadly. His teeth were stained red with betel-nut juice. Brand nodded, not sure whether he was being mocked.

The twelve soldiers were correctly dressed by the time Brand returned to them: battle order with blanket roll. Alone on the empty platform they fidgeted nervously and stayed close together. Between the platform roofs a rectangle of pale raspberry sky flickered with bats.

'Transport's coming,' said Brand.

'How far from here is Amritsar, Sarge?' asked Private Tarrant, the company know-all. His voice was as hoarse as a smoker's cough and it sounded unnaturally loud in the silent twilight. Brand was surprised that Tarrant didn't know where it was. Or at least pretend to know.

'We came through it on the train,' said Brand.

'We were talking about the trouble there last year,' said Private Palmer, 'when the Gurkhas opened fire on

187

the crowd.' Palmer had a Mons Star and had fought from 1914 until 1918. He was a quiet man who said everything in the tone of doleful prayer. Strange, thought Brand, the varying effects of war upon a man's character. It made some men into maniacs and some into monks.

'They left the wounded to die,' said Tarrant.

'Gurkhas,' said Johnson. He was a tall man with a big, Old Bill moustache. His skin was as brown as the furniture of his rifle. 'They just kept firing into the crowd. About four hundred killed and over a thousand wounded.'

'The Colonel in charge was court-martialled,' said Tarrant. He spat at the rail and hit it. Tarrant had a large, mauve, drinker's nose, its motley surface made uglier by the pitted scars of syphilis. He touched his nose self-consciously.

'Bullshit!' Johnson said. 'One of the English newpapers got up a subscription for him. He collected twenty-six thousand quid.' For a few minutes they all tried to comprehend such a sum of money.

'Roll on my bounty,' said Tarrant.

'What will you do with your fifty pounds?' asked Private Peel, the youngest man in the detachment. He had joined up in 1918 and had seen only four weeks in the trenches before Armistice Day. He had eight more years to do.

'I'm going to buy a little pub,' Tarrant replied.

'You'll need a bloody sight more money that your fifty pounds bounty,' said Johnson.

'I got a little bit put away,' said Tarrant smugly.

Johnson stroked his big droopy moustache and winked at the others. 'Then I wish you wouldn't bloody come on the tap so often.'

'Now then, lads. Let's have you!' said Sergeant Brand as he heard the sound of the 3-ton Dennis echoing down the empty main street. The headlamps flashed in the glass-fronted shops to make a kaleidoscope of light patterns as it stopped with a squeak of brakes outside the railway-station booking hall. The soldiers' boots and rifle butts clattered on the polished stone floor and echoed among the silent ticket counters and offices. They seemed determined to make as much noise as possible when letting down the tail flap and helping each other up into the lorry. Sergeant Brand slotted the tailboard chain into place and took his rightful seat beside the driver. There was no windscreen, and the movement of air was cooling as the lorry rumbled along at its maximum speed of twelve miles per hour. Brand settled back into the hard seat and braced his boots against the jolting of the solid tyres upon the cart-rutted road. This was familiar to Brand; half his life had been spent lumbering around the world in these old Dennis lorries. In the back the soldiers held tight to the metal frame to keep their balance. Young Peel and Tarrant stood on the kit and tried to see what was ahead.

The headlamps picked up gnarled trees and the red dusty verges of the parched land, and reflected back enough light for Brand to see the driver's badges – South Wales Borderers – and his pinched face. The driver sensed Brand's attention and looked round anxiously.

Brand said, 'Your mob stationed here?'

'No, thank Christ. Just this week. It fair gives me the creeps. I wouldn't do your job for a pension.'

'You'll know better about that,' said Brand, 'when you are within two years of getting your pension.'

The driver nodded. All the soldiers were long-service regulars, he'd noticed. Some of them had campaign ribbons from the 'nineties. They were specially chosen men, perhaps. He glanced again at the Sergeant. On his chest there was a slab of ribbons. Not just Mutt and Jeff, Frontier and Durbar, but real medals: an MM and a DCM, too. The driver had spent his entire war service in

Cardiff and he often wondered what it would have been like in the front line.

'You must have shot plenty of people in the war, Sergeant.'

'Hundreds, laddie,' said Brand airily. It wasn't at all the answer for which the driver had hoped, but he decided against pursuing the subject. Brand smiled grimly; he knew exactly what was in the driver's mind.

At the village they stopped. Brand sniffed the warm air. Usually there was a bustle of arguments and laughter, an atonal opera of musicians, vendors, orators and scribes. Not since the last epidemic had Sergeant Brand been in a village so dark and silent. It was on a slight incline. From here they could see hundreds of miles across the dark plains where other villages flickered in the rising air like swarms of fireflies. But here there were no lights, no sounds either, no cry of jackals nor stray village dogs. Even the army bungalows were dark. When the tailboard banged down, a treeful of monkeys awoke and made a high-pitched din, but they were soon quiet again.

'Move off,' said Brand. 'Follow the path to where you see the light.'

The soldiers moved in single file along the bullock track. They crossed another road and saw the entrance to the cantonment, and beyond that the bazaar. That too was dark and silent, and two white regimental police were on duty to guard it against thieves.

Brand halted his men outside the guardroom and waited patiently at the counter. He could see right through the Orderly Room to an office where two Indian informers, an interpreter and an SWB officer were arguing softly. When they saw Brand the officer closed the door. It was almost five minutes before the Orderly Corporal arrived. It was unbearably hot in the guardroom. The punkah wallahs had been evacuated with the other natives so that the woven rush flaps were now stopped for the first time in many years. The still air smelled of perspiring bodies and there was a haze of tobacco smoke which was part of everyone's attempt to repel flies.

'Where's the canteen?' asked Brand.

'Wet canteen is closed,' said the Orderly Corporal. 'No one can get a glass of beer until tomorrow. You'll get a penny cup of tea in the dry canteen, though. It's better than the Mess.'

The dry canteen was run by the Royal Army Temperance Association. Tarrant had an argument about taking his kit and rifle inside. The others had left their equipment in the guardroom but Tarrant decided that it wasn't safe there.

The guardroom staff had assigned a couple of men on jankers to prepare beds in the prison building for Sergeant Brand's unit. The privates were sleeping on palliasse beds made up on the ground, three to a cell. Sergeant Brand had a charpoy and a cell to himself. They brought him an oil lamp which cast a light across the stone wall and revealed a filigree of prisoners' graffiti.

'Leave the door open,' he joked to the Orderly Corporal, 'I'm claustrophobic.' The lamp attracted the flies and insects until his mosquito net was shivering with their movement. Brand extinguished the light and sat smoking his pipe until the small hours when there was no sound anywhere, except of the rats in the rafters. Finally he slept.

They were awoken at 5 A.M. with the pint mugs of hot sweet tea. The jankers men brought it. 'That's the one good thing about working in a prison,' shouted Tarrant, 'there's always plenty of labour.' He sang tunelessly to test the echoes of the small cell. He was even more pleased when the Orderly Corporal came back with a jar of rum. The VC mixture, Tarrant called it.

Palmer was going to have some, too, but the smell of it suddenly reminded him of the tot they were given immediately before going over the top during the war. Several of the others found their memories of the smell equally disquieting, but only Palmer declined to drink some. Tarrant drank Palmer's tot.

Sergeant Brand tapped out his boots with the automatic action that all residents of the tropics learn. Pooglui Prison had been built a century before and was infested with beetles and bugs. They fell to the floor as the soldiers shook out their blankets. Palmer took his tea into the courtyard. It was the violet darkness that precedes dawn, and already the air was perfumed with the promise of searing heat. A couple of hawks were circling, hoping to eat before the sun drove every living thing to seek cover. There were two armed sentries on the gate and three on the roof of the main building. The jankers men carried out two Mess tables, put them end to end at one side of the yard and piled them with sandbags. Palmer glimpsed faces at some of the cell windows but they dodged aside when they saw him looking up. He swallowed his hot tea and told himself he'd soon be back on the train.

It was cold standing in the yard; the stone prison walls never became warm. Tarrant was the only sensible one of them. He'd put two wollen pullovers on under his jacket. Brand had asked for permission for his men to wear overcoats, but there was a Major on duty in the guard-room in the morning. Everyone there was irritable. The Major yelled 'No' without even looking up at him.

'Rude bastard,' thought Brand. He knew the type. The boys had shot one like that as they went over the top during the Third Ypres.

At first Brand couldn't make out what the sound was: it couldn't be a swarm of bees. Finally he realized it was men reciting the rosary; the whole prison must have been chanting it together. Then he came out. The prisoner was in dirty khaki drill. There were no laces in his boots, so he had to shuffle along to keep them on his feet. There was a military warder on each side of him. They had rifles, with fixed bayonets, over their shoulders. It was difficult to know whether they were holding his arms to press him forward or to hold him back; perhaps they were just gripping him tight out of compassion.

Behind the prisoner came the priest in surplice and stole. He was talking all the time. Once one of the escort nodded and seemed to repeat what the priest had said. The escort looked more frightened than the prisoner. There were others behind them: a Provost Sergeant, the Colonel of the regiment and some officers, probably witnesses.

When the Provost Sergeant hurried around the prisoner, pulling a black bag from his pocket, the people at the front halted and all the others blundered into them as though they weren't looking where they were going. The Provost tried to put the black bag over the prisoner's head, but he said, 'I don't want that, I will die like an Irishman.' The others began to argue and there was almost an exchange of blows, but the priest said, 'It's for the sake of the firing-party, don't you see, now?' The prisoner put the black bag on.

About this time two of the jankers men carried a chair into position by the far wall. Iron bars were tied to its legs making it too heavy for one man to manage. When the prisoner got to the chair he pulled off the black bag, which caused the Provost Sergeant to run forward in great excitment.

The boy said, 'But I only wanted to look around, Father.' It was the priest who put the bag on his head again. Then the priest leaned close to him and gave him Absolution. Everyone heard the boy say, 'May the good God receive my soul,' in spite of his voice being muffled by the bag. Still with the bag over his head, the boy emptied his pockets; he gave the priest some annas, cigarettes and a green silk handkerchief. Then he gave him the farewell letter that the other Irish prisoners had sent to him the night before.

The priest put rosary beads over the boy's head and said, 'Jesus, Mary and Joseph, I give you my heart and my soul.' The boy cried briefly with shallow sobs like a small child that is not hurt and not really expecting comfort.

The Medical Officer was making tutting noises by then, and the Colonel undid his overcoat and looked at his pocket-watch. The Provost Sergeant came to the back of the chair and began to rope him to it. 'I'll not be tied down,' said the boy angrily.

The priest pushed the Provost Sergeant aside, and grudgingly he folded up the rope. The Medical Officer wanted to remove the rosary and a scapular of the Sacred Heart that the priest had pinned to the boy's tunic. He had a small paper target to pin over his heart instead. The priest took the target and pinned it over the scapular. Then they all stood aside and looked towards Sergeant Brand.

It was sun-up by now. Its light made the upper storey of the prison a rampart of shining gold and yet the courtyard was as cold and blue as a deep pool of water. In this gloom the men moved slowly, like deep-sea divers, and like bubbles their breath rose white above them. One of the officers from the guardroom had a white handkerchief in his hand. Brand nodded to his men and they picked up their guns from where they were resting on the sandbagged table. No orders were spoken. Each man sighted on the white target.

Brand looked back to see his firing-party. Twelve good men and true, like a jury. They stood warped and crippled in the unnatural pose of marksmen, like trees bent before a gale. Each held his rifle tight to shoulder to avoid the pain of recoil. Their faces were pushed askew against the wooden rifle butts and each man had one eye screwed up tight, the other bright and unseeing. Here was Tarrant, who lived solely for his cheap beer and weekly visit to the brothel. Here was Johnson, his large greying moustache twisted between cheek and rifle butt like a strangled rat. Ex-cowherd Johnson, who in France had milked cows into the ground rather than see them in discomfort, now cradled a trigger in the same forefinger and would squeeze it with the same merciful caress. Here was poor dead Palmer, killed on the Somme in 1916, who had continued to parade and be paid and stand unremarked among his live comrades ever since. Palmer was the best shot, but would he aim? And here was Peel, shorter, younger and more determined to be a man than any there. He, 094 Private Peel, would align the sights and squeeze the trigger, discharge the spent warm cartridge and pour two pints of boiling water through the barrel, exactly as regulations prescribed.

'Fire,' said Brand, but no word came. 'Fire,' said Brand silently, hoping that they would shoot and kill and leave him neither stained by the thing that he must do, nor responsible for not doing it.

It was the Provost Sergeant that gave the order. He'd long since decided that Brand would not have the guts for it. It was always the same with these bemedalled bastards. And such was the tension that no one knew that it was not Brand's voice. Even Brand himself for ever believed that he had spoken the command, it screamed so loud within his mind. He saw the sunlight inching down the wall, so fast did the sun top the mountains.

'Fire!' The birds screamed and the blood spurted as Palmer's bullet punctured the paper target, the Sacred Heart and the real heart, too; where the others went made no difference. The priest ran towards the writhing body and, ripping the bag from his head, anointed the

195

still-moving boy with holy oils. The body was jammed upright in the chair, its boots in a spreading pool of blood. The birds that had screamed and beat upon the air when the volley rang out circled the courtyard, their wings making a deafening clatter and their shadows darkening the sky.

A voice called, 'May his soul rest in peace.' It was a solemn voice, loud and clear. The firing party turned to see the cell windows crowded with the faces of other Irish soldiers, their faces gilded like those of the temple gods. Seeing their buttons and badges, a prisoner shouted, 'The Royal Fusiliers did it, the Royal Fusiliers!' The voice echoed on the high walls.

'Party atten – shun!' Brand marched them out of the prison yard. 'Left, right, left, right, left, right. Pick 'em up there. Swing your arms. That man, that man, left whe – el.' The men marched as they had never marched before, concentrating upon perfection, each man's mind with no other thought.

The railway station was transformed by blinding sunlight. It was suffocatingly hot. The thirteen Fusiliers emerged from the refreshment room wiping their beery mouths, elbowing and cursing their way to the platform's edge. They dragged their packs, water bottles, blankets and rifles into a heap and stood around it, making a little island of khaki in a sea of black faces and white garments. The soldiers were quieter than usual: bovine, almost, like men who had done a long day of hard labour.

Brand could taste the salt of his own sweat. Across his back he wore a great cross where the straps of his equipment had left damp stains of perspiration. Every soldier wore the same mark.

'What did he do, then?' said Tarrant. He broke a stick of tobacco, put a piece in his mouth, rewrapped the remainder and tucked it into his small pack.

196

Johnson waited to be sure that he wasn't going to offer it around. 'Bit late, asking now, ain't you, Tarrant?'

'Irish,' said young Peel. 'The whole regiment wanted their ticket . . . on account of the Black and Tans knocking their families about.'

'Oh well,' said Tarrant, heaving a sigh of relief on finding it was a crime to which he was not likely to be tempted. 'Can't have that, can you.' The chewing tobacco made his speech difficult to understand.

'Poor buggers.' Palmer worked the bolt of his rifle a couple of times. It was clean and freshly oiled now. Palmer's Enfield was better cared for than any in the battalion. He stroked it proudly.

'Can't have what?' Brand asked irritably.

'Let the Paddies have home rule, Sarge,' explained Tarrant patiently. 'Next thing the Gyppos would want it, then the rest of the bleedin' Arabs would start . . .' He laughed as another thought came to him. 'Next thing you know we'd have the bloody Indians telling us to *inshi*.' He spat a generous gob of tobacco juice at the sun-hot rail. It sizzled. Several Indians respectfully noted his marksmanship.

'That's why they evacuated the wogs from the village, eh?' said Johnson. 'In case they turned nasty?'

'Good idea,' said Tarrant.

It troubled Brand that the army high command and Private Tarrant were in accord. Two years was going to be a long time to wait, Brand decided.

The train came in very slowly. Hundreds of white-clad natives hung all over it. The locomotive shrieked and disappeared in a cloud of steam. The crowded platform became a bedlam of farewells, advice and fierce struggling for space aboard the train. The Fusiliers maintained a dignified calm, as befitted European soldiers.

The smiling railway official appeared at Brand's elbow. He passed the soldiers' packs through the window and sternly reprimanded the natives who were sitting in compartments clearly marked RESERVED FOR ARMY OF INDIA.

'Here today, gone tomorrow, sahib,' he shouted, and smiled his red, toothy smile as the train began to move.